AUTHOR'S NOTE

Although Cameron, Asher, and Jason attend real American colleges, all names, events, and processes are used fictitiously and are in no way based upon, or reflect, any existing staff, events, or processes.

THE ENDGAME IS YOU

A RIXON RAIDERS EPILOGUE

L A COTTON

THE ENDGAME IS YOU

Copyright © L A Cotton 2020
All rights reserved.

Edited by Andrea M Long
Cover by Lianne Cotton
Images licensed from: Shutterstock and Adobe

RIXON RAIDERS

The Trouble With You
The Game You Play
The Harder You Fall
The Endgame Is You

PROLOGUE

Cameron

"This is the life," Asher said as he laid back on the lounger, folding his arms behind his head.

He wasn't wrong.

His family's place in the Hamptons was something else. We'd been out here before, him, Jason, and me, but this time was different. Better. This time we had our girls with us, and it was our final summer together before we went off to college. Hailee and I were heading to Michigan next week to get settled before classes started. Then Jason and Felicity would be moving to UPenn in a couple of weeks, with Asher and Mya across the river at Temple University.

It was the end of an era. No more Raiders, no more high school, but a new adventure.

I flicked my eyes to Jason who was sat in a chair, elbows propped on his thighs, chin resting on his fists. "They'll be okay, you know." I chuckled, sliding my gaze to where the girls were currently dipping their toes at the water's edge.

"It's not them I'm worried about," he grunted. "It's them." Jason tipped his head to where a group of guys were checking out our girlfriends, clearly unaware that we were sitting in wait.

"You need to lighten up." I gave him a pointed look. "Soon we'll be at college and you know there's going to be plenty more where that came from."

"Ugh, don't remind me." Jason Ford, prodigal son of football and Rixon's golden boy pouted.

"For real, you're worried about college dick?" Asher asked. "Felicity has your tattoo on her skin. She's not going anywhere."

Jase reared back. "Of course she's not fucking going anywhere. But it's college. Coach Hasson ran a tight ship, but it'll be a whole other level at college. I can't expect her to sit around and wait for me."

"Well, no, she'll probably do that thing called make friends. I've heard all the kids are doing it." Laughter rumbled in Asher's chest.

"Fuck you." Jase kicked his lounger and Asher almost went flying.

"You're really going to have to learn to rein in Mr. Possessive Asshat, you know?" I said.

"Just put a ring on it, then every fucker will know she's taken."

"Don't be stupid, he's not going to—" My brows pinched. "Jase, man, please tell me you're not actually considering it. We're eighteen."

"Like you wouldn't put a ring on Hailee's finger in a heartbeat."

He had a point.

But we had time. I wanted us to both enjoy each other first. Fuck knows we'd earned it.

Jase shot up out of his seat. "He's dead."

"Whoa." I leaped up after him, blocking his way forward. "They're talking." Glancing back, I watched the group of guys laugh with the girls. It seemed harmless enough... until one of them made a beeline for Hailee.

"Let's go," I growled, possessiveness streaking through me.

"I guess I'd better come make sure the two of you don't do something stu—Oh, hell no." Asher whipped off his sunglasses and gawked in their direction, watching as one of the guys offered to put lotion on Mya's shoulders.

"I'll take the two on the left." He barged past us. "You two take the others."

Hailee

"Come on, don't be like that. Just because you got guys waiting for you doesn't mean we can't hang out."

"Is this asshole for real?" Mya arched a brow.

"Bitch please, you should—"

"Oh, hell no, you did not just call her a bitch." Flick stepped up to the douchebag and glared at him. "My boyfriend would kick your ass all over this beach."

"I'd like to see him try." The guy laughed, glancing at his friends who chuckled.

"That can be arranged," Jason, Cam, and Asher closed in around them.

"Oh, hey, babe." Flick grinned. "This is Tom. He was just telling us how he thinks we should ditch you guys and hang out with them instead."

Mya shot me a knowing look. Flick was a bit of a loose cannon where Jason was concerned. It was crazy, but she loved his possessive alpha side. She said it got her all hot for him, so I was hardly surprised she was enjoying this.

"Flick," I warned, because while she might have enjoyed seeing her guy get pissed, it usually didn't end well for everyone else.

Cameron moved around us, pulling me into his side. "Hi." He smiled down at me as if we were the only two people on the overcrowded beach.

"Hi." My fingers splayed over his hard abs, loving how warm his skin felt. "We should probably intervene," I whispered, "before he does something stupid."

Jason was all up in the guy's face, eyes narrowed dangerously. "I suggest you take a walk, now."

The air crackled around them and I silently willed the guy to walk off. This was supposed to be a relaxing weekend before we all went our separate ways. I didn't want to have to call Kent to bail his son out of county jail for assault.

Thankfully, the douche must have recognized the emergence of Jason's dark side because his hands went up. "Shit, yeah, man, my bad." They started backing up.

"Yeah, you'd better run," Flick yelled.

"Seriously," I said. "Do you have to provoke him?"

She shrugged, launching herself into Jason's arms. "It's all the testosterone. It gets me hot."

"Gets you wet more like." Jase nipped her bottom lip before capturing her lips with his.

"I love you guys, but that was too much information," Mya grumbled.

"Jealous, babe?" Asher prowled toward her. "Because I'm pretty sure I can help you out with that."

"Asher, don't you dare." She backed further into the water's edge.

"You should know not to dare me by now. I never lose." He winked before diving at her. One minute Mya was standing there, the next she was over Asher's shoulder, shrieking like a banshee as he ran straight toward the ocean.

"He's so gonna get it," I said around a smile, watching as Asher dropped her into the water.

"He's gonna get something all right." Jason barked out a laugh.

"Why is everything about sex to guys?"

"And girl." Flick snickered, holding up a finger.

I rolled my eyes, unable to smother the laughter building in my chest as Jase dipped my best friend and smothered her with wet, sloppy kisses.

Despite all his alpha ways, they were so freaking cute. Even if she had completely lost her mind and let someone tattoo 'Property of a Raider' on her skin. But that was Felicity Giles, a girl who loved with her whole heart and lived every second like it was her last. I was excited for them to go off to UPenn and chase their dreams. Even if Cameron and I would be a nine-hour ride away in Michigan.

"You okay?" Cam looped his arm around my neck and gazed down at me.

"Yeah, I'm good."

I had great friends.

The most perfect boyfriend.

And our whole lives ahead of us.

Cameron

"We're lucky bastards, you know that, right?" Asher tipped his beer toward where the girls were laughing and talking, sipping the sugary sweet cocktails Felicity had insisted on making.

After a day at the beach, we'd headed back to the house. The place had a grill too mammoth not to put to good use. A cloud of smoke currently drifted into the sky as Jase flipped burgers and steaks.

"Yeah, I know." Hailee caught my eye and smiled; and fuck, if it wasn't like a bolt of lightning to my heart.

I loved that girl. I loved her more than I had ever loved another person, and the thought of starting my life with her should have been the happiest moment of my life. Except I had a gnawing guilt over leaving Rixon, of leaving my mom and dad and my kid brother, Xander. Mom was better, she was, but it didn't stop the trickle of fear I felt every time I imagined being a nine-hour ride away and getting a call that she was sick again, or that Xander was having bad nightmares still.

I wanted to be there for them, always. But Hailee

wanted Art School, especially STAMPS at the University of Michigan, and she deserved it.

She deserved it so fucking much.

"You all set to be a Wolverine?" Asher asked.

"I guess."

"Don't sound too excited about it."

"It just won't be the same, ya know?" I took a long pull on my beer.

"Yeah, being a Raider was something special, a once in a lifetime experience. But college will be good, you'll see."

I wished I could be as laidback as Asher. Even after everything he and Mya had been through with her ex, and with his mom getting shot, he still managed to paste on a trademark Bennet smile.

I envied him. His ability to dust himself off and embrace everything life had to offer.

I wanted it; I did. But fear held me back. Fear about the future... about everything changing.

Rixon was my home.

But Hailee was my heart and I knew I'd follow her anywhere.

"Yo," Jase yelled over his shoulder. "Steaks are almost done."

"And that's our cue to get the salad," Felicity mumbled.

"And the sauce. Don't forget the hot sauce." Asher smirked. "Oh and bring some pickles and some of those—"

"Babe," Mya clipped out. "You have legs."

"Yeah, but I'm supervising Jase."

I snorted at that.

"It's a good thing I love you." She rolled her eyes playfully before taking off after the girls.

"I love her so fucking much," he said, as if it was the simplest thing in the world.

But I got it.

We all did.

We were young. Three guys chasing their dreams of football, fame, and fortune. But we'd already found our forever girls.

And that was worth everything.

Every fucking thing.

Hailee

"I am stuffed." Felicity sat back rubbing her swollen stomach.

"You'll be stuffed later," Jason smirked.

"Is that a promise?" Desire glittered in her eyes.

"Guys, really?" I groaned, and Cameron squeezed my hand, fighting a smile.

"What?" She shrugged. "We're all friends."

"Damn right, we are."

Jason reached for his beer and thrust it in the air. "No matter what the next four years bring, you'll always be my best friends."

"Aww, love you too." I poked out my tongue at him and everyone laughed.

"You're not so bad, Raine."

"Likewise, Ford."

It was hard to believe there had been a time when Jason and I couldn't stand one another. He still drove me crazy sometimes, but I loved him like a brother. He was fiercely protective of those he cared about, and that now included me.

"But seriously, guys, we might not be Raiders anymore, but we will always be friends. Distance won't change that."

"Easy for you to say," Cam said, glancing between Jase and Asher, "you'll be a stone's throw away from each other."

He chuckled, but I heard the strain there. Cameron was coming to Michigan for me, for *my* dream, and I couldn't help the tiny pang of guilt I felt. He reassured me all the time it was the right move, but I didn't ever want him to regret it.

Or resent me.

My shoulders sank.

"Hey." He squeezed my hand and I lifted my eyes to his. "I'm joking... it was a joke."

"I know."

"You think he'd really go anywhere you're not?" My stepbrother asked me.

"Jase," Flick warned.

"It's okay," I said, forcing a weak smile. "Nine hours is nothing. We can still see each other at the weekend and at holidays."

"Damn right we can." Asher tipped his beer at us. "Nothing, not college, distance or time, is going to ruin this."

His words settled over the six of us, turning the air thick with anticipation.

College was a big step. Things would change. *We* would change.

But was Asher right?

Were the bonds between us strong enough to survive?

PART I

———

Sophomore Year

1

Jason

"Okay, gather round," Coach Faulkner called us in, and we fell into position around him. Shoulder to shoulder, teammate to teammate. The anticipation of a new season was thick in the air. Last season, as a freshman, I'd been so close to tasting victory, but in the end it had been Cornell who took the title.

It had been a bitter pill to swallow. I wanted to be the best, to win, to prove myself.

But this year... this year it was ours. We were thirsty for it: training harder, pushing harder. I might have only been with the Quakers for a year, but I felt at home here. We had strong leadership, a strong defense, and one of the best offenses in the whole damn country.

It was our year to bring that trophy home.

So the grim line on Coach's face had a pit carving through my stomach. Something was about to happen. Something that affected the team.

Fuck.

"I've got some news, ladies, and you're not going to like it." He yanked off his Quaker ball cap and rubbed a hand over his jaw. "Manella is out."

A collective grumble filled the air.

Lincoln Manella was our running back, our fucking captain. It was his senior year; he was supposed to be entering the draft next spring. He couldn't be out.

"Just got word from his old man. He tore his ACL and needs surgery."

"Fuck," I breathed, flicking my eyes to my friend Gio. His lips pulled into a thin line.

This was bad.

Very fucking bad.

"So, what's the plan, Coach?" Jared Galloway, our starting fullback and one of the senior players, asked.

"We need a new captain."

All eyes slid to me.

"Whoa." I held up my hands and stepped back, bumping into the player behind me. "It should be an upperclassman."

There were guys on the team who had more seniority than me, more experience. Just because I'd arrived last year a true freshman, taking the QB position from the senior player before me, didn't mean I'd wanted or been qualified enough to be the captain.

"It should be you, son." Coach tipped his chin in firm reassurance. He believed in me, he trusted me... and it floored me.

I'd led my high school team, carried that responsibility with pride and tenacity. But this was different.

This was college.

"I agree," Jared said. "You more than proved yourself

last year, Jase. You might only be a sophomore, but this is the right call."

"Anyone got a problem with this?" Coach scanned the fifty young men surrounding him and not a single one of them stepped forward to disagree.

"Decision made. Congratulations, son." A small smirk graced Coach's rugged face. "You just became our fearless leader."

The team broke out into a chorus of hoots and hollers as everyone congratulated me on the promotion. But I stood there blindsided, completely in shock, with only one thing on my mind.

I did not see that coming.

Felicity

Hot wet lips trailed up my neck, kissing and biting, teasing. A soft moan spilled from my mouth, lulling me from my nap, as I tilted my head, welcoming the delicious sensations.

"I missed you," Jason whispered against my throat.

"It's only been a few hours."

Even if it felt like more.

"It's too many." He let out an exhausted sigh, tucking my body into the hard curves of his.

"What time is it?"

"Six thirty."

"Crap." My eyes flickered open. "I was only supposed to have a twenty-minute power nap."

"Long day?" he asked, nuzzling my neck again. I loved it, the feel of Jase's five o'clock shadow rough against my soft skin, his arms wrapped possessively around my body as if he might never let me go.

And I didn't want him to.

This guy owned my heart and soul and I didn't ever want it back.

"Yeah," I admitted. It was only two weeks into the semester and classes were already kicking my ass. I shuddered to think how intense things would get in junior year once clinical practice started.

"You've got this, babe." Jason nibbled my earlobe sending volts of electricity shooting through me. "You just need to believe in yourself."

"I actually signed up for some extra tutoring."

"You did?" I felt him tense behind me.

"I almost failed last year, Jason." My brows furrowed, disappointment sitting heavy in my chest.

"But you didn't," he reminded me.

"No, but this year is only going to get harder."

I thought my love of animals, dedication to animal welfare, and determination to succeed was enough. Turns out, it wasn't.

"Hey." Jason shuffled us so that I was on my back and he was leaning over me. "You've got this." He slid his fingers into my unruly curls and kissed me, his tongue curling around mine, stirring my body to life.

"I have some news too," he breathed the words against my lips.

"Tell me." I cupped his face, pushing his away gently so I could look into his eyes.

"Linc had an accident. He's out for the season."

"Oh God, Jason, that's awful." Lincoln had really taken Jase under his wing last year, so I knew how hard this would hit him.

"That's not all..." He hesitated, a flash of fear streaking across his eyes. "Coach wants me to be captain. He thinks I'm ready."

"Jason..." I smiled so wide my cheeks hurt. "That's amazing. I'm so freakin' proud of you." I slung my arms around his neck and crushed him to me, peppering his face in sloppy kisses. "My boyfriend, QB One *and* captain of the Penn Quakers."

But he didn't revel in my excitement. He was still and quiet.

Too quiet.

"Jase?" I held him at arm's length. "What is it?"

"What if I'm not ready? What if I screw it up? Fuck, you should have seen the way they were all looking at me. As if I had the answers, the power to make things happen."

"Babe, listen to me and listen good. You, Jason Ford, are one of the best quarterbacks in the country right now. You came into a well-established team and proved yourself in your freshman year. You ranked *third* for the most passing yards in a single season." Pride flooded me. "Third, babe. That's huge. Not to mention the fact you blew the Quakers passing yards record out of the water."

Jason was already in the Penn Quaker Hall of Fame;

he'd already made Quaker history. But with that kind of accolade came the pressure to always do more, to constantly be better.

"You've got this, Jason," I said with complete conviction, ignoring the niggle of doubt that this was going to take my boyfriend away from me even more than football already had.

Didn't captains have to spend more time with the coach, watching game footage and devising plays? And then there would be the rest of the team. The captain was a leader, a father figure, the guy everyone went to when they needed an ear to listen or a shoulder to lean on.

But if anyone deserved it, it was Jason.

So how could I even contemplate feeling anything besides pride for him?

The answer was, I couldn't.

I knew what football meant to him. Jason had given everything to the game he loved. Hours of conditioning and practice. He was one hundred and ten percent committed to his team, to forging a successful football career for himself. And I was the lucky girl who got to stand at his side and watch him flourish. So I stuffed down my reservations, plastered on my best smile, and said, "I'm so proud of you."

"And I'm so fucking lucky to have you in my corner." Jason captured my lips in a slow, deep kiss. The kind of kiss that we sank into, exploring each other's mouth with easy familiarity. But like every time we touched, it soon turned into more. Heat simmered between us, rising into an inferno neither one of us could control.

Jase slid his hands to the hem of my t-shirt and began working it up my body. His lips brushed a path up my stomach, his tongue dipping into the valley of my breasts as he pushed the material over my head.

"God, Jason," I moaned, jamming my fingers into his thick, dark hair. He continued painting my skin with his lips, tracing letters of love and promises of forever over my chest and collarbone.

"I need you."

He pulled away, leaving me cold, to yank off his jersey. My eyes traced over his body, his chest, shredded with muscle, all hard lines and deep grooves.

"Sometimes I forget how gorgeous you are," I whispered, reaching out to touch him.

He'd always been physically fit, a sculpted work of art thanks to all the conditioning and hours spent in the gym. But since playing college ball, his body had matured and refined in a way that left me breathless every time I saw him naked.

"You look like you want to devour me." He smirked, holding my heated gaze with his own.

"I do," I confessed.

Jason dived for me and we became a clash of limbs, fighting to undress the other, desperate to touch and feel and taste. I was hardly surprised he got me naked first, pinning me to the bed and dipping his head to flick his tongue over my nipple. I cried out, arching into his mouth. His smooth chuckle reverberated around my sensitive skin, sending shivers skittering up my spine.

Nothing would ever compare to this, to the feel of him

touching me... owning me. I loved it, almost as much as I loved him.

"I want to take my time," he rasped as he punched his hips forward rocking into me, "but I'm not sure I can."

"So don't," I practically pleaded. We could play afterwards. Right now, I needed to feel him inside me, above me, riding me hard and fast until neither of us knew where I ended and he began.

Jason ripped my panties off; ripped them clean off my body before sinking inside me without warning. We both groaned, his hands tangling with mine either side of my head. "I love you, Felicity, so fucking much."

"Then show me..." My voice cracked as he pulled out and rocked forward again, sheathing himself deep inside me.

Jason loved like he played football. With complete determination, skill, and confidence. He knew exactly how to play my body, the way he played on the field, and he knew exactly how to make me come every damn time.

"Fuck, babe, nothing... *nothing* will ever feel as good as this." He thrust into me again, over and over, splintering my body apart in the best kind of way. Jason kissed like a man starved, dragging the oxygen from my lungs and taking it for himself. One of his hands slipped down my thigh, hitching my leg higher, letting him drive deeper.

"Jason... God..." I breathed, trying to ground myself, but it was too much.

It always was.

"Let go, babe." He kissed me slower, mimicking the shallow rock of his hips as he drew pleasure from my body.

My legs began to tremble, sweat beading on my skin and slipping down my body. I pressed my lips together, trapping the moan building into my throat. I was so close.

"I can feel you, Felicity, feel you squeezing my dick." He whispered the dirty words against my ear as I unraveled. "Come for me, babe. Come all around my..."

I shattered around him, crying out his name, over and over.

Jason flattened himself against me, slamming into me with renewed vigor as I rode the lingering waves of pleasure.

His body locked up tight, his jaw tense with concentration as he jerked inside me.

We lay there, silent and sated and I'd never felt happier. We'd had an amazing freshman year together, and now we had three years of living as a couple, in a cute little off-campus apartment a few minutes' walk away from Penn.

But no matter how happy I was, how madly in love with Jason I was, there was always a little voice of doubt in the back of my mind.

Jason was already Quaker royalty. In one season he had won the hearts of his teammates, coaches, and fans. And now he was captain. He would soon be thrust into the public eye more than ever.

No matter how hard I wanted to believe in the fairytale, the truth was he would always be in the spotlight, and I would always be the girl at his side in the shadows.

But it was something I was just going to have to learn to

live with, because giving this up—giving *him* up—wasn't an option for me.

Ever.

2

Felicity

Veterinary medicine was both my dream and nightmare. I loved animals. I loved them with every fiber of my being. There was something about being surrounded by crates of four-legged friends that brought me peace, and it had been at A Brand New Tail in Rixon that my dream to become a vet had been born. However, the truth was, I was barely staying afloat. The course was naturally science-based but I'd underestimated just how hard it would be to stay on top of multiple classes. This semester alone, I was studying general pathology, parasitology, and microbiology.

If I wanted to stay on track, I needed help.

Which is why I'd signed up for the tutor program.

Butterflies zipped around my stomach as I headed for the Hill Pavilion. I was meeting Darcy for coffee nearby and to discuss a schedule. All tutors were fourth year or post-grad students, and I was hoping she could help me keep my head above water this year.

But when I reached the coffee shop, I saw no sign of her. I checked my watch. I was almost five minutes late. Glancing around the place again, I decided to wait by the noticeboard. It was chock full of advertisements for roommates, social clubs, and local bars hosting live music nights.

Someone tapped my shoulder and I spun around. "Can I help you?" I frowned at the guy.

"Felicity Giles by any chance?"

"Um, yeah."

"I'm Darcy, your tutor." The guy smiled and my eyes widened.

"*You're* Darcy? But I thought..." I stopped myself. How rude and presumptuous I'd been.

His smile grew timid. "You thought I was a girl?"

"Sorry." My cheeks pinked.

Darcy shrugged. "I'm used to it. Unfortunately for me, my mom had a strange affinity for Jane Austen in her younger years." He held out his hand. "It's nice to meet you."

"That's... I really don't know what to say." My awkward laugh echoed around the high ceilings.

"Shall we?" He motioned to one of the tables. "I already got myself a coffee. What would you like?"

"Oh no, you don't have to do that. I'll just—"

"Felicity, relax. I can afford to buy coffee for a pretty girl." His eyes twinkled.

"I have a boyfriend," I blurted out. God, this was beyond awkward. I bet he thought I'd lost my mind.

"Good thing I'm only here to tutor you then. What's your poison of choice?"

"Latte, please," I conceded. "Cream and sugar."

He gave me a reassuring nod before heading for the line

while I got comfortable at the table. My phone pinged and I dug it out of my bag.

QB#1: Hope tutoring goes well.

Me: Just arrived. Shouldn't you be practicing, Captain?

I smiled.

QB#1: You can tell Darcy from me that she'd better take care of my girl.

The knot in my stomach tightened. Jason thought Darcy was a girl, just like I had when I pulled one of her—*his*—tickets off the advert pinned to one of the course noticeboards.

Crap.

He wasn't going to like this. It wasn't about *not* trusting me. Jason had a problem trusting anyone with a dick around me. But it worked both ways. If I knew Jase was getting tutoring from a girl, that he was spending a lot of time with someone who wasn't me, I'd be jealous too.

It was just the way we loved each other. Deeply. Obsessively. Completely.

Darcy chose that exact moment to return, placing my latte down in front of me. "I didn't know if you'd eaten or not, so I grabbed two blueberry muffins."

"I already had breakfast, but thank you."

"Hey, more for me, right?" His smile was easy, his eyes warm. Darcy didn't give off creeper vibes. He was nice, friendly, even if a little forward.

"So, Penn Vet, how's that going for you?"

"I want to say it's a breeze, but then I wouldn't be sitting here."

"Yeah, freshman year can be a shock to the system, but it gets easier, I promise."

"Why do I feel like you're sugarcoating the truth?" Our laughter swirled around us. "Thanks, for the latte." I brought the glass to my lips, reveling in the bittersweet smell of cream and coffee beans.

"Anytime. So why don't you tell me what you struggled with last year and we can look at your classes for this semester and figure out a plan of action."

"Sounds good." Some of the tension left me. Darcy was my tutor. This was strictly a business relationship. Jason couldn't get pissed about that. Besides, he knew I was his.

I felt a lick of determination skitter up my spine. I needed this if I was going to be able to survive sophomore year. I needed help.

And Darcy Bannerman came highly recommended.

After almost two hours, and a rigorous plan, Darcy and I packed away our things and left the coffee shop. "So I'll see you Wednesday?" he said, waiting for me to move ahead of him.

"Sounds good," I said, ducking around him and stumbling straight into—

"Jason?"

"Hey," he shot me a smile that made my knees weak. "How was tutoring?" His arms went around me, as he dipped his head to kiss me.

"It was good. I... uh... this is Darcy, my tutor." I wriggled free of his grasp to step aside and introduce them.

The second Jason's eyes landed on Darcy his expression darkened. "*You're* the tutor?"

"Darcy Bannerman." He held out his hand. "You must be the boyfriend."

Jason narrowed his gaze, staring at Darcy's hand as if it was contagious.

"Jase." I hissed, elbowing him in the ribs.

"Jason. Jason Ford."

"As in starting quarterback Jason Ford?" Darcy's brow went up.

"Felicity didn't tell you?"

I rolled my eyes at that.

"No, it never came up."

"Okay," I rushed out. "This has been fun and all, but if you'll excuse us, Darcy, I need to talk to my boyfriend about the etiquette of conversation." He chuckled as I pulled Jason away. "What the hell was that?" I hissed once we were out of earshot, marching down the street.

"You failed to mention your new tutor was a guy." Jason fell into step beside me.

"That's because I didn't know."

"Yeah, I suppose Darcy is a pretty girly name."

"Jason." I glowered at him. "Is this going to be a problem?"

"Will you get a new tutor if I say yes?" His brow arched in challenge. I wanted to believe he was joking.

I knew he wasn't.

"If I'm going to pass this year, I need all the help I can get, and Darcy comes highly recommended."

"I bet he does," Jason grumbled, his eyes going over his shoulder, but Darcy was long gone.

Usually, I loved this side of him. Possessive and dominant. But now he was just being stupid.

"Jason, look at me." I stopped, gripping his jaw, forcing his eyes to mine. "There is nothing to worry about."

"And if our roles were reversed. If it was me spending time alone with a tutor who just so happened to be a hot girl?"

"You think Darcy's hot?" I hadn't really noticed.

"Don't push me, Giles."

Giles.

A shiver ran up my spine. He only called me that when I'd really pissed him off.

"I'd hate it, okay? But I would trust you. Because that's what you do when you love someone. You trust them."

His hard expression melted away, giving way to something that looked a lot like regret. "Shit, Felicity, I trust you, I do." He pulled me into his arms, brushing his nose over mine.

"I know you do." My hands curled into his Quakers hoodie. "But I need this Jase. I need to get a handle on classes before I sink too deep."

"And he's really the best?" He studied me.

I nodded.

"Okay," he breathed. "But if he so much as looks at you the wrong way, I will—"

"Ssh, my Neanderthal." I kissed him softly, but Jason took control, sliding his hands into my hair and slipping his tongue past my lips.

"Get a room, Ford," someone yelled, and we both turned to find a group of football players.

"Are you guys working out today?" I asked.

"Yeah. With Linc out—"

"I get it."

"Tonight. Me, you, and our favorite takeout?"

My smile fell. "I'm volunteering at the shelter."

He mumbled his displeasure under his breath.

"I won't be late. Why don't you hang out with the guys at The Gridiron and I'll meet you afterward?" The sports bar was on my route home from Paws, the animal shelter I helped at sometimes.

"Yeah?"

I nodded, and Jason leaned in capturing my lips again. "I know I'm a lot," he whispered, "but it's only because I'm so fucking crazy about you."

Love wrapped around me like a warm blanket as I fisted his hoodie tighter. "The feeling is entirely mutual."

"Yo, Ford," Gio yelled. I liked him. He was American-Italian and hailed from Verona County in Rhode Island. He had an adorable habit of cussing in Italian. It wasn't any wonder they called it the language of love; his accent was so freakin' dreamy.

"Yeah, yeah, Abato," Jase shouted back. "That's my cue." He stole another kiss. "I'll see you later."

Pressing my lips into a small smile, I nodded. "Go show them who's boss, Captain." I smirked. Jason chuckled, giving me a flirty wink before taking off toward his friends and teammates.

I watched them jostle him, fist bumping and laughing. He looked so happy, so free. He'd slipped into college life with ease. Even with his intense athletic schedule, he was doing well in his classes and keeping up with the workload. Nothing fazed him.

Unlike me, who had almost failed my freshman year.

I shook off the feelings of inferiority. This year would be better. This year I would give my studies everything, and now I had Darcy in my corner, everything would work out.

Except as I headed for my first class, I couldn't stop the seed of doubt taking root in my stomach.

Jason

"What's up, man?" Gio asked as he spotted me on the weight bar. "You seem... tense."

"Felicity got a tutor."

"And that's a problem wh—" Realization dawned on his face. "The tutor is a guy?"

My jaw clenched as I pictured that fucker's face. I didn't know him from Adam, but I already didn't like him. He'd be spending time with Felicity. My woman, the other half of my fucking soul. Possessive asshole or not, I was not okay with some guy spending quality time alone with *my* girl.

"It's just tutoring." He snorted. "You don't have anything to worry about."

"Don't I?" My brow rose.

Felicity was gorgeous. All seductive curves and wild spirit. I saw guys around campus watching her, wishing they could have a taste. They soon backed the fuck off when they saw me, but still.

"Seriously, bro, Fee wouldn't look twice at another guy. She doesn't get all crazy possessive when we hang out with the cheer squad."

Oh, she did. I just didn't advertise the fact. Freshman year, Felicity had almost attacked a girl for trying to get my number at a party. Instead, I'd dragged her to the nearest bedroom and fucked the anger right out of her.

Our love was like wildfire. It burned constantly. Throw water on it and it simmered to a gentle flicker, but add a strong wind and it became an inferno. Ferocious and unpredictable.

"This is why I don't have a girlfriend," Griffin joined us. "Too much drama for my liking."

"Dude, you don't have a girl because you're a walking,

talking STI." Gio exploded with laughter but it became muted when Griffin punched him in the arm.

"I had chlamydia once. One fucking time. She told me she was—"

"Rule number one, Griff," I said. "Always wrap it."

"Yeah," he dragged a hand through his hair, "And what's rule number two?"

"Get a steady girl and then you won't have to worry about wrapping it."

Gio and I shared a knowing smile. He wasn't in a serious relationship like me and Felicity, but he had steady pussy.

"Nah, I need to sow my wild oats before I settle down." Griffin grabbed some free weights and started pumping.

"You just haven't met the right girl," I said. I didn't make a habit of sharing my personal life, but Gio and Griffin were my closest friends on the team. Both juniors, they'd taken me under their wing last year. It wasn't the same as having Cameron and Asher—guys who had known me most of my life—in my corner, but I trusted them. And sometimes, when I needed to, I confided in them.

"You guys want to get a drink at The Gridiron later?" I asked them.

"Fee giving you a free pass?" Gio smirked and I flipped him off.

"She's working a shift at the shelter. She'll meet us after. I'm going to invite Asher and Mya too."

He'd been nagging me to get together, but it had been a crazy couple of weeks.

"I'll ask Jordan if she wants to come."

"Pussy whipped." Griffin coughed under his breath.

"We're friends."

"Friends with benefits," I corrected.

"Yeah, I guess."

"Count me out," Griffin said. "But enjoy couples' night." He squeezed Gio's shoulders before heading for the chest press.

"I hope his dick falls off."

I chuckled. "He just hasn't met—"

"The right girl, yeah." Gio looked conflicted but I didn't ask. If he wanted to talk about Jordan, he'd bring it up. "How are you feeling about being captain?" He changed the subject.

"It's an honor." It was. I'd come to Penn wanting to go all the way, and this was just another step in the right direction.

"But..." he prompted.

"Linc left some big shoes to fill."

"Nah, you've got this. If it wasn't going to be this year, it would have happened when he graduated. This spot was yours the minute you stepped foot into the locker room."

"Thanks, man, I appreciate it."

"No need to thank me, Jase. You're one of the best; the kind of leader this team needs to go all the way. I have faith in you, man, even if you don't."

"I guess we'd better get to work then." I smirked, brushing off his compliment no matter how much it meant to me.

"Yeah." He chuckled. "We'd better."

3

Felicity

"Fee, baby, get over here."

"Asher?" I smiled, surprised to see him standing at the bar next to Jason and... "Mya!"

A high-pitched squeal broke from my lips as I bypassed Asher to go straight to his girlfriend. "It's so good to see you."

"Girl, it's been three weeks."

"Three weeks too many." I hugged Mya tighter, uncaring that she preferred to keep PDAs to a minimum. "Tell me everything. How are classes? The new place? I want to know it all."

"Are you okay?" She eyed me with suspicion.

"What? I can't be happy to see one of my best friends?" I smiled, but it felt weak.

"Don't worry about me or anything," Asher grumbled, making Jason, Gio, and Jordan laugh.

"So needy." I locked my arms around his neck and hugged him. "It's good to see you, Ash."

"Not as good as it is to see you." He held me tight until familiar fingers pried me away.

"Okay, put my girl down, Bennet, before I have to snap

your fingers and ruin your football career before it even gets started."

Asher released me and Jase pulled me between his legs. "I missed you."

"I want to say I missed you too, but the shelter had two new rescues, Pug puppies... they were so cute."

"Great, I've been axed for goddamn dogs."

"Aww, you still own my heart." I kissed the corner of his mouth. "But these were some really, *really* cute puppies."

"Well if you'd rather stroke those than..." he whispered the words only meant for me as he trailed a finger down my neck. A shiver rolled through me and I swallowed a whimper.

"Didn't think so." Jason kissed the end of my nose. "Hey, Hugh, get my girl a drink," he called over to the bartender.

"Sure thing. Your regular, Fee?"

I nodded. "So, what have you guys been talking about in my absence?"

"Oh, you know, trying to deflate this one's head since he got promoted to captain." Asher pinched Jase's cheek, and he batted him away. "How does it feel to wear the crown?"

"Asher," Mya sighed.

"He knows I'm proud. I'm like the proud brother he never had. But that shit's got to weigh a ton."

"I was born ready," Jason said, but I saw the tightness in his eyes. He was having doubts about his ability to lead.

We all knew he had nothing to worry about though because he *was* born ready.

"That's the spirit, bro." Asher clapped him on the shoulder. "Now Fee is here, we should toast."

"We don't need to—"

"To Jason," he thrust his beer in the air, "may your leadership be firm and your game strong. Congratulations, man."

Jason

I tried to heed Asher and Gio's words. Every day we practiced, every day we studied game tapes and devised new plays, I tried to hold onto the fact that I'd waited for this day my entire life. But with the opening game finally here, I couldn't deny I had a constant gnawing in my stomach.

It didn't help that Felicity was spending more and more time with tutor boy. She was finding one of her classes, parasitology or something, particularly difficult. But it wasn't like I was around much to help, or even could if I was.

The team had become my life the last couple of weeks. Everything building to this moment.

"Okay, ladies, look alive." Coach Faulkner moved through the locker room, fierce determination etched in the lines of his face. "Tonight, we're going to go out there and show everyone why it should have been us bringing that trophy home last season, you hear me?"

"Yes, Coach." Our battle cry echoed off the walls, reverberating all the way down to my soul. Hunger pulsed inside me as adrenaline trickled through my veins. No synthetic high could ever replicate this; the moment you stepped out on that field. The second we became gods among men: worshipped and adored, immortalized in the chants of the crowd, every sigh and gasp and cheer. It was our oxygen, our life-force. And I would let it fuel me, push me harder and faster until we won.

"Number one," Coach fixed his eyes on me, "you ready?"

It was the million-dollar question.

I felt strong.

One hundred percent on form.

But I also felt humbled; honored to captain my team, to walk them into battle and lead them to victory.

Because losing was not an option.

"I feel ready, Coach."

"Glad to hear it, son. Dartmouth are looking strong, but they don't have our heart. They don't have our drive or our thirst." He jabbed his finger into the air. "They don't have what it takes to go all the way. Bring it in."

The sound of our cleats against the locker room floor was like the beat of a drum.

"Quakers on three. Jason, do the honors."

I punched my hand into the middle of the tightly knit circle as fifty other hands followed suit.

"One... two... three... Quakers."

We broke formation to file out on the field. I grabbed

my helmet and jogged ahead, my heart racing, blood pounding between my ears. But it was nothing compared to the roar of the crowd as we jogged out onto Franklin Field.

"Soak it up, man," Griffin yelled around a shit-eating smirk.

And I did. I slowed to a walk, soaking it up. There had been something special about playing in my freshman year. But this, being here as captain, was the pinnacle of my football career to date. I needed to take a minute, to allow myself a second to process everything. My eyes scanned the VIP section and found Felicity. She was grinning from ear to ear, sitting beside Jordan who was here to support Gio on a 'purely platonic' basis. I called bullshit, but whatever. I could just make out Felicity mouthing the words, "I love you."

In that moment, with my girl in the bleachers, the thirteen-thousand strong crowd all shouting my name, I felt like a god. Worshipped. Adored. Loved.

I felt unstoppable.

This was my calling, my domain... my kingdom.

And I was born to rule.

Felicity

"Oh my god," I breathed as I watched Jason fall back, search the field for his wide receiver, and send the ball flying toward him. He caught it, tucking it into his body and sprinting toward the end zone.

"Go, go," Jordan yelled, and the entire crowd seemed to yell with her.

"Touchdooooown," the announcer's voice filled the stadium, and everyone went wild.

"They've got this," Jordan said around a big smile.

"Yeah." I dropped down in my seat and searched for Jason. He was celebrating with his teammates, high-fiving and fist-bumping. He looked completely at home out there, as if he was born to play.

I didn't doubt he was. Some people possessed that natural talent, a destiny written in the stars. We were watching football greatness unfold right before our eyes, and I didn't think there was a person in the crowd who doubted that Jason Ford, a boy from a small town in Pennsylvania, would one day grace the NFL with his talent and charisma.

The cheer squad broke into a sideline celebration and I smothered a groan.

"Hey, turn that frown upside down." Jordan nudged my shoulder.

"They're just so obvious." I heard them talk about Jason, watched them lust over him despite the fact everyone knew he was off the market.

"Please tell me you're not worried about the likes of Shelly and Farrah?"

"She wants him." Shelly Halstead had wanted Jason since the first day he stepped foot on campus.

"Half the girls here want him."

My lips pressed into a thin line, but Jordan only laughed.

"He loves you; everyone can see that. You have nothing to worry about."

I liked Jordan. She was one of my few girlfriends here. It wasn't that I'd purposefully avoided making friends during freshman year, just it was hard when your boyfriend was the new football star. Girls either looked at me as the competition or they were brazened enough to try to use me as a steppingstone to get to Jason and his friends. I'd quickly given up trying to form genuine friendships. I had Jordan and Mya, and I spoke to Hailee all the time despite the nine-hour distance between us.

"It's just... a lot," I whispered the confession, hating myself for even saying the words.

Jason gave me no reason to worry. He was unwavering in his love for me. But as I watched the team celebrate; watched the cheer squad lick their lips and bat their eyelashes in his direction; listened to thousands of people chant his name; I couldn't help but think the very thing he loved would one day be the thing that drove a wedge between us.

Jason was going places.

And I barely had my head above water.

Jordan pulled me into a side hug. "You and Jason are endgame, Fee. I see the way he watches you, the way he tracks your every move. That guy is head over heels in love with you. All this: football, the crowds, the high; it would mean nothing if he didn't have you by his side."

As if he heard her words, as if he felt the doubt swirling around me like a storm cloud, Jason looked up, searching the bleachers for me. I couldn't see his eyes behind his helmet, but I felt them.

And I couldn't ever imagine *not* feeling them.

———

The party was wild. But there was something about winning the first game of the season that had everyone worked up. Jordan and I lingered on the periphery with a couple of the other girlfriends, sipping our sugary sweet mixed drinks, while Jason, Gio, Griffin, and a handful of their other friends took shots.

"Okay, okay, let me get up here." Griffin jumped up on the huge breakfast island and ushered the crowd into silence. "I think I can speak for everyone when I say we were all fucking bummed when Coach gave us the news about Linc. But I think I can also speak for everyone here when I say we never doubted Jason would be there to pick up the pieces." He fixed his eyes on Jase and raised his beer in the air. "I'm proud to call you my friend, man, but I'm even prouder to call you my captain. And I know... I just fucking know, you're going to take us all the way this season."

The room exploded with cheers and hollers, quickly turning into chants of, "Speech, speech."

Jason cleared his throat, looking more than a little displeased at Griffin's little stunt. "Those of you who know me, know I'm a private guy, so I'm going to keep this short. Linc is a good guy, one of the best. He took me under his wing last year and guided me right, and for that, I owe him. I'm fucking honored to lead the team in his stead. To Linc."

He tipped his beer forward and nodded at his rapt audience.

"Linc." The name echoed through the room, a somber reminder of how fragile this life could be. How, one minute, you could be on the cusp of football greatness only to have it all ripped away in the blink of an eye. Or, in Linc's case, a simple wrong landing during a basketball game with his younger brothers.

Jason's eyes found mine across the kitchen, and he stalked toward me.

"We're going to dance," Jordan announced, shooting me a knowing glance.

I gave them a small wave, heat coursing through my veins as Jason drank me in. I was wearing skinny jeans and a fitted Quaker tank top, no different than half the girls here. But the way he looked at me... it was as if I was the only girl he could see.

The only girl he wanted to see.

"Hey." He crowded me against the counter.

"Hey." I smiled. I couldn't help it. Jason would always bring out the best and worst of me. "Nice speech."

"You know I fucking hate doing that."

"I know." I ran my fingers over his jaw. He didn't resemble a twenty-year-old sophomore. He was all man. Tall, broad, and muscular with a five o'clock shadow over his angular jaw, Jason had graduated Rixon a boy on the verge of adulthood and matured into a confident, self-assured guy who knew without doubt what he wanted from life.

"Congratulations, QB One." Fixing my mouth over his,

I kissed him. Jason groaned against my lips, tangling his tongue with mine and sliding his hands into my hair.

"Fuck, babe, no win will ever taste as good as this."

His words made my heart swell, even if I knew he was just caught up in the moment.

Because for as much as I wanted to believe I came before football... part of me wasn't so sure.

4

Felicity

I woke up alone, again. It was the third morning in a row. Jason seemed to spend every spare second he had in the gym, or with his coaches, or cramming in extra study hours so he didn't fall behind in his classes.

The Quakers were on a winning streak and no one wanted to lose momentum.

Grabbing my cell off the nightstand, I smiled at the text message from Jason, but it didn't quite reach my eyes.

It never did these days.

QB#1: Sorry... I know I promised to be there this morning, but the guys texted wanting to get an hour at the gym before classes. Everyone is feeling tense about the game Friday.

Me: Go do your thing. I can't wait until tonight xo

· · ·

Wednesday night was always date night. We didn't always go out, but we always cleared our schedules for each other. Sometimes we went across the river to hang out with Asher and Mya, sometimes we caught a movie downtown, or sometimes we stayed in and just enjoyed a slice of quiet in our crazy lives.

QB#1: Tonight? Shit, I told the guys we'd get together to watch the tapes from the game last week.

My stomach sank. He'd forgotten about date night.

Me: Oh, okay. Well, I could always use some extra hours studying. We can take a raincheck.

QB#1: I'll make it up to you, I promise.

Me: I know xo

I did. Jason would strive to lavish me with a romantic meal at our favorite restaurant or a seductive night in, worshipping every inch of my body until I'd forgotten all about his indiscretion.

Except, the further into football season we got, the less time we spent together, and the more my heart ached.

———

"Whoa, who died?" Darcy chuckled as he greeted me at the coffee shop.

"Huh?" I frowned.

"The glum face? Is everything okay?" He ushered me to a table.

"Yeah, I'm fine."

"You know, I'm a good listener as well as an excellent tutor."

"Modest too, apparently." I managed a weak smile.

"Let me guess, guy troubles."

"How did you—" I stopped myself. The last thing I wanted was to discuss Jason with my tutor.

"Nine times out of ten, it is." He shrugged as if it wasn't a big deal, but something told me it was. "Want to talk about it?"

"Not really, no." I pulled out my notebook.

"You know, I wouldn't have put you with Mr. Hotshot Football Player."

"What is that supposed to mean?" My defenses went up.

"I just meant... football players usually attract a certain type of girl."

"You don't know anything about me or Jason, Darcy." I really didn't appreciate his tone or the insinuation in his words.

"Sorry, this is coming out all wrong." He ran a hand through his hair. "All I mean is, I've been on campus long enough to witness my fair share of heartache." There was something in his tone... something personal.

"You don't like the football team very much, do you?"

"I guess you could say that." His expression hardened.

"They don't all fall into the typical jock stereotype, you know?"

"I'm sure there are exceptions to the norm."

There were. Jason, Asher, Cameron, even Gio, and Griffin—for all his goofy ways—were good guys. They played hard and they loved hard.

"But..."

"But I guess I don't understand how intelligent, independent, ambitious girls are so willing to be second string to a sport."

I didn't know what I'd expected... but it hadn't been for him to pick up on my insecurity.

"When you love someone, Darcy, you support their passions, their hopes and dreams." It came out harsher than I intended.

"I can see I hit a nerve. I didn't mean—"

"Jason and I love each other very much. He supports my dreams and I support his."

Why was I justifying myself to him? I didn't owe him or anyone else an explanation about why I was with Jason.

You didn't choose love, it chose you, and Jason Ford had stolen my heart a long time ago.

"I'm sure he's a good guy." Darcy finally opened his notebook.

"He is."

I'd wanted to come to our tutor session and focus on something else besides the gnawing pit in my stomach. But now there was an awkward tension in the air as Darcy talked me through the life cycles of protozoan parasites.

We worked like that for an hour, in stilted conversation potted with thick silences.

I'd never been more relieved when he announced we were done. I hurried to pack up my things and abruptly stood.

"Felicity, wait," he said. "I owe you an apology. My prejudices about the football team, are just that, mine. I watched a couple of my good friends get hurt pretty badly by jocks... it left a sour taste in my mouth. I'm sorry."

"I appreciate your words. But I meant what I said, Darcy. You don't know anything about mine and Jason's relationship." And I intended on keeping it that way.

"You're right, I don't. As long as you're happy, right?" He gave me a goofy smile, but it was like a punch to the stomach.

Because I wasn't happy lately.

"Same time Thursday?"

I hesitated. I could request a different tutor and hope they had even half as much as knowledge and Darcy's ability to break down the science and explain it in a way that I understood.

But that felt like the coward's way out.

He was entitled to his opinions, even if they had hit a sore point.

I gave him a small nod and said, "I'll see you then."

Jason

"You think we're ready?" Griffin asked me as we filed out of the room adjoining the locker room. We'd been watching game tapes from Dartmouth's game against Yale last week. They were the team to beat. The team we needed to beat to stay at the top of the league.

"We're ready," I said with complete confidence. Since our opening game, we'd gone from strength to strength. Being quarterback always gave you a natural leadership role in a team, but now that I was captain, something had clicked. We all felt it. But it was more than that. I had something to prove. To myself, Coach, the team, the fans... Linc.

I needed to take them all the way.

Anything else was *not* an option.

"We're heading over to the house if you want to come for a beer?" Gio said.

He and Griffin lived with a few of the other guys in a big house just off campus.

"Not tonight." I wanted to make it home in time to see Felicity.

Between classes, the team, and her work at the shelter, we'd barely seen each other. I wanted nothing more than to take my sweet time exploring her body before I sank deep inside her.

"Hot date?" Griffin smirked and I flipped him off.

"Actually, I missed date night." Guilt snaked through me. But I could make it up to her. I couldn't, however, make it up to the game Friday night if we weren't ready.

"Oh shit, you're gonna be in the doghouse, man."

"Nah, Felicity understands." But as I said the words, my stomach knotted. I was asking a lot of her. We both knew the level of dedication and discipline playing college ball would require, but even I'd underestimated just how intensive it would be. Playing for the team didn't only mean practice and games. It meant bonding with the guys, being a brotherhood... a family. You couldn't just shirk your way out of that. Especially not when you were the captain.

"I'll catch you later," I said to the guys as we filed out of the building. It was already dark.

I jogged to my car and climbed inside. Then I checked my cell. There was a text from Cameron, but nothing from Felicity.

With a heavy sigh, I fired up the engine, backed out of the parking lot and took off toward our building to make it up to the girl I loved more than I ever thought possible.

———

Our apartment in Powelton Village was less than a ten-minute ride. The closer I got to our building, the more I couldn't help but feel like I'd messed up. Wednesday was always date night. It was something we'd started back in freshman year, to make sure we put aside some time each week for the two of us to just be Jason and Felicity.

I pulled into my allotted parking spot and cut the engine. It was almost nine thirty. Late, but not too late to salvage the night.

Grabbing my cell, I found Cameron's number and hit dial.

"What did you do?" he asked.

"How do you know I did anything?"

"Because it's nine thirty on a Wednesday night..." He let the words hang.

"I think I messed up tonight." I dragged a hand over my face.

"It can't be that bad."

"It's date night and it slipped my mind."

"That doesn't sound so scandalous." He chuckled.

"I'd arranged to watch game tapes with the guys, so when I realized, I—"

"You chose the guys over Felicity."

Fuck. The fact he answered for me only cemented my guilt.

"When you say it like that it does sound like a dick move."

"Fee knows the deal. She knows what it means to be on the team."

"Yeah, I guess..."

Silence fell over the line until Cam said, "Things are okay between the two of you, right?"

"Yeah, I think so. I mean, we're not spending much time together lately. She's at the shelter or with tutor boy.

And I'm either trying to study or with the team... Why? Has she said something to Hailee?"

"What? No! Even if she had I'm not sure she'd tell me."

I scoffed at that. "Bullshit. My sister would tell you everything."

"Did you just refer to Hailee as your *sister*?"

"No," I grumbled at my slip of the tongue.

"You did. I heard it as plain as day. You said—"

"Okay, Chase, don't get too excited. It doesn't mean anything."

"Oh, but it does." I heard his smile. "Wait until I tell her you've progressed to sis—"

"I'm hanging up now."

"I'm sorry." His laughter subsided. "Your secret stays with me, I swear."

"Hmm. I should never have called you." That's what I got for seeking out some advice.

"Yeah, you should. You needed someone to tell you to pull your head out of your ass, go find your girl and grovel."

"You're right." That's exactly what I intended on doing.

"Are the girls still planning to take Mya away for her birthday?"

"I think so," I said. "Asher suggested we could go stay with him."

"I'm easy. It'll be good to see you."

"Yeah, you too. Thanks for the chat."

Cameron's laughter filled the line again. I was fucking

ecstatic that he found this funny. "Anytime. Now go grovel."

We hung up and I climbed out of my car, grabbing my bag from the trunk. Our apartment was on the top floor with views of the Schuylkill River.

When I got inside, it was quiet. "Babe?" I called.

Throwing my keys onto the sideboard, I moved deeper into the apartment. The lonely plate on the draining board made my chest tighten. She'd eaten alone.

It shouldn't have mattered as much as it did.

Felicity

I heard Jason before I felt him. Measured footsteps in the hall, the creak of the bedroom door, the rustle of him stripping out of his clothes. Part of me ached to glance over my shoulder and greet him. But the part that had stewed all night on Darcy's words kept me rooted in place, eyes closed and heart heavy.

The covers moved behind me and a rush of cool air hit my back, and then Jason's hard, warm body brushed mine. "Babe, you awake?" He slipped his arm around my waist and tucked me into the lines of his chest. Usually this was my happy place, but tonight, the distance between us felt bigger than ever.

What was happening?

We'd survived freshman year. That was supposed to be a couples big test, wasn't it? Survive freshman year—the lure of new experiences and endless parties—and you could survive anything.

Jason's lips ghosted over my neck, trailing a path to my ear. "I'm sorry," he whispered, and those two words damn near broke my heart. They were so full of regret and sincerity, but they didn't promise the one thing I really needed to hear.

That it wouldn't happen again.

Jason

We were leading the Ivy League four to none, with three games left to play. The pressure was on after what could only be described as a flawless season. Probably my best football season to date. My passing yards total was already a season best and I was currently tied second with a kid out of Cornell on the Division I FCS season passing yards leaderboard.

I was heading for the single most perfect season of my life... and yet, my personal life was a fucking mess.

Letting out a frustrated breath, I pushed open the door to the hotel bar and found Asher and Cameron sitting in wait.

"Hey, it's good to see you." Cam got up first, pulling me into a guy hug. Seeing my friends was like coming home. I loved my team at Penn: the guys, the coaches, the fans; but it wasn't Rixon.

"Sorry I'm late."

"Don't sweat it, we know the drill." They did. They'd seen me captain the Rixon Raiders, witnessed how deep I became when handed such a responsibility. I didn't just carry my own thirst for the win, I carried every single player's.

"Everyone is on edge. This could be a perfect season—Penn's first in almost a decade. It means a lot to the team, to Coach."

"And it should," Asher said, taking a long pull on his beer. "Just don't let it go to your head."

"Fat chance of that." Cam shot me a smirk, and I flipped him off.

"Between classes and the team there isn't time to let it go to my head, trust me." The bartender pushed a beer toward me, and I nearly drained the thing in one.

Fuck, I needed this. A night shooting the shit with my friends; friends who didn't want to talk plays or game tapes or team stats.

The girls had gone to a fancy spa in Michigan to celebrate Mya's birthday in style, while we'd decided to join Asher at his place. Thanks to his sizeable trust fund, their apartment building was like a five-star hotel, complete with a fully equipped gym, bar and restaurant, and roof top terrace.

"So, I was looking at your stats," he piped up. "You know Heisman could come knocking this year."

I snorted. "There hasn't been a Heisman Trophy winner come out of the Ivy League since the fifties."

"It could happen. You're dominating ESPN chatter."

Yeah, when hell froze over.

"I'll just be happy to see us maintain our perfect record and win the league."

We fell into easy conversation. Time and distance

didn't sever our bond. If anything, our friendship was stronger than ever.

"So my mom is having a Thanksgiving thing," Asher announced. "She's keeping it low key. She wants to invite Kent and Denise; your mom, dad, and Xander," he said to Cameron.

"Yeah, sounds good. What about Mya's aunt?"

He let out a weary sigh. "It's a work in progress. She and Mya got into it the other week, don't ask me what about. Probably me or the fact that Mya is getting too involved in her studies."

"Isn't that supposed to happen?" I asked.

"Yeah, but she's volunteering at a community project and she comes home with all these stories about the kids..."

"She wants to save them all," Cameron said, and Asher nodded.

"And she can't, ya know? I'm just worried she'll get too attached."

"Nah, she's strong," I said, "and she wants to help. There's nothing wrong with that."

Mya had grown up in a rough neighborhood. She'd witnessed firsthand what deprivation, crime, and drugs could do to a person. So the fact she wanted to be a social worker and try to make a positive impact was commendable.

"Says the guy who's been spending more time with his team than his girl." Asher's brow quirked up.

"She's always with tutor boy." I bristled. Darcy's name was becoming a regular mention in our conversation. I fucking hated it, but it wasn't like I could complain, not when Asher was right. I was spending more time with the team than Felicity. But it was only for another few weeks. Once the season was over, things would settle. We could be us again.

"Dude, you're not seriously jealous about a guy who enjoys talking about animal science all day?"

"You're forgetting that Felicity also likes talking about that stuff."

"He's her tutor. You're her... person."

Cameron chuckled. "He's right, you know. You and Felicity are going the distance. All couples have highs and lows."

"Well being in a low fucking sucks."

"You're still... doing it, right?"

I gawked at Asher. "What are we, five?"

"I'm just trying to help." He shrugged.

"Yeah, well maybe we should change the subject." Dissecting my relationship with Felicity was making me cranky.

"If you make it as one of the Heisman finalists, we can take a trip to New York for the weekend to celebrate."

"Seriously, Ash, the chances of me getting shortlisted are almost non-existent." I rubbed my jaw.

"Still, I'll ask my old man if we can reserve the penthouse for the weekend. That way, even if you don't shortlist, we can still go, but it can be a commiseration instead of a celebration." A shit-eating grin tugged at his mouth.

"There's something very wrong with you," I grumbled.

"But you love me."

Yeah, I did. He might have been like sunshine on a fucking rainy day, but Asher was my best friend. Cameron too. Almost fifteen months had passed since we left Rixon for college, but they were still my guys.

Always would be.

He pulled out his cell phone and I frowned. "What are you doing?"

"Texting my dad."

Cameron smothered a chuckle and I rolled my eyes. "Of course you are."

Felicity

A weekend with Hailee and Mya had been just what I'd needed. We'd spent an entire day and night being pampered and primped, finishing off the day with cocktails in the tropical al fresco style bar. This morning we'd enjoyed a champagne breakfast and then gone our separate ways. Mya and I had flown back to Philadelphia together.

"Oh my god," she murmured as we came through arrivals to find Asher holding a huge 'welcome home' sign. "He did not."

"Oh, he did." Laughter spilled from my lips. I scanned the arrival lounge for Jason, my heart sinking when I didn't spot him.

"My two favorites." Asher approached us.

Mya grabbed his face and squished her nose against his. "It's a good thing I love you."

"What, you didn't like my sign? It took all morning to paint."

"You have completely lost your mind."

"Fee, baby," he kissed Mya before stepping around her, "get over here."

"Hey, Ash." I gave him a hug. "Have you seen Jason?"

"Actually, he asked me if I minded giving you a ride."

"He did?"

I dug out my cell phone checking my messages again. Nothing.

"He got caught up and didn't want to keep you waiting. Come on, the Jeep is out front." He grabbed Mya's overnight bag and started toward the door. But I hesitated.

"Hey," Mya said. "I'm sure he wanted to be here."

"Yeah."

I'd confided a little to Mya and Hailee about how strained things had become between Jason and I lately, but I hadn't wanted to put a dampener on our time together. Besides, they had both found their feet at college. Hailee and Cameron had a group of friends they regularly hung out with, and Mya was friends with a ton of her fellow social work classmates. It seemed like it was only me who, a year later, still hadn't slotted into college life.

We piled into Asher's Jeep and I sat quietly in the back while Mya caught him up on our time at the spa. My cell burned a hole in my pocket. I wanted to text Jason and ask why he hadn't been able to pick me up, but I didn't. Because I was pretty sure I already knew the answer.

It was only a fifteen-minute ride to Powelton Village. Asher rolled to a stop outside my building and twisted around to face me.

"Thanks," I said.

"Anytime. Don't be too hard on him, yeah?"

My brows pinched. Wasn't he supposed to side with me? After all, Jason had abandoned me at the airport in favor of hanging out with the team.

"I'll see you both soon."

"Don't be a stranger," Mya said around a warm smile.

I climbed out, dragging my small suitcase behind me. Usually, I'd be excited to see Jason after time apart, but the permanent knot in my stomach only twisted tighter.

Asher honked his horn and I waved, watching as the Jeep disappeared into the steady stream of traffic. There was no sign of Jason's Dodge Charger in the parking lot, and my heart sank a little more.

I rode the elevator up to the top floor, silently planning a hot bath and comfort food. But when I stepped inside the apartment, the gnawing pit in my stomach was replaced with butterflies. A vase of red roses greeted me, a card propped up against the glass. I plucked it up and opened it.

Felicity,
   Be ready by 7.
   Wear something sexy.
   J

I couldn't have fought the smile pulling at my lips if I'd tried. It didn't fix everything, and I knew we still needed to talk, but it was exactly the sign I needed.

———————

Ninety minutes later, the knock at the door made my heart flutter in my chest. I opened it gently, hardly able to believe my eyes. Jason looked devastating. The slim-fit dark jeans hugged his muscular thighs, and the black dress shirt molded to his broad shoulders and thick arms. He'd left the collar open and rolled the sleeves to his elbows. His hair hung over his eyes a little, in the way I loved so much.

Sweet baby Jesus, he stole my breath.

"Hey." A faint smirk played on his lips as he let his eyes glide slowly down my body and back up again. I'd opted to wear a tight sweater dress that finished just below my knee. It skimmed my curves and scooped low on my chest. Demure yet sexy. Although from the heat in Jason's gaze, I felt stripped naked.

"Fuck," he breathed, leaning in to brush his lips over my cheek. "You look stunning."

"You don't look so bad yourself."

"I'm sorry I wasn't at the airport. I wanted to surprise you and I knew Asher could give you a ride home."

Home.

I loved hearing him refer to our apartment as home. It was so intimate, so permanent. It made it easy to forget the last few weeks and how strained things had been between us.

Jason tucked a curl behind my ear, letting his thumb brush my cheek and hover over my bottom lip. "I really, *really* want to fuck you right now."

"Jason." My breath caught, desire pooling in my stomach.

"But I made reservations, so that will have to wait." He ran a hand down his face, torment glittering in his eyes as if he wasn't sure.

"We could always stay home?" I batted my eyelashes.

"As tempting as that sounds, I have some making up to do. Dinner *then* sex." He fixed his mouth over mine. It was hard and bruising and a promise of things to come. A shiver ran down my spine as I melted into him. "I know things have been hard, but I love you, Felicity. So fucking much."

Jason

It took everything I had not to drag Felicity into the bedroom, strip the ridiculous sexy dress from her body and make love to her. Need pulsed through me as we kissed. My fingers slid into her silky strands, loving how soft it felt against my skin. She smelled amazing, like a vanilla and strawberry sundae. I wanted to taste her, trail my tongue up and down her body until she was a writhing mess beneath me.

Fuck, I wanted her.

It made me realize how much we needed this. We'd still been having sex. I was a hot-blooded guy and Felicity had a body built for sin. But I couldn't remember the last time we played. Spent hours exploring each other's bodies, finding new ways to make each other come undone. We were both busy, both exhausted by the time bedtime rolled around.

"What?" Felicity whispered, uncertainty shining in her eyes as I studied her.

"Just thinking how much I've missed you."

"I've missed you too." She curled her freshly painted nails into my shirt.

"Well, tonight is ours," I said with confidence, threading our hands together.

"I can't wait." She smiled up at me, and my heart beat harder.

That single look... it was everything. And I knew that no matter how hard or demanding college got, we'd be okay. Because this girl—this beautiful, intelligent, driven woman —was mine.

6

Jason

The Rooftop was a fancy restaurant with incredible views of the city. The floor-to-ceiling windows made it feel like you were dining under the stars, even if it was too cold to sit out on the terrace.

"That was amazing," Felicity let out a contented sigh as she placed down her silverware.

"I thought we could have dessert to go."

Her cheeks pinked as my mind filled with images of her laid out beneath me. "Jason, stop." It came out a little breathless.

"What?" I smirked. "I'm not doing anything."

"You know exactly what you're doing." Her brow went up.

"Excuse me," a voice said, and I shot the balding guy approaching our table an irritated look. "I hate to disturb you, but are you Jason Ford?"

"He is," Felicity answered for me.

"My son is a huge fan. He'd never let me hear the end of it if I told him I saw you and didn't ask for an autograph."

Fuck. He wanted to do this now? When I was thinking

about pulling Felicity into the nearest bathroom and eating her for dessert?

"I wouldn't usually ask, but my son, well, he's sick. It's been a tough year and I just know this would make his day."

Double fuck.

"Here." Felicity leaned over and handed me a clean napkin while the guy thrust a pen into my hand.

"What's your kid's name?" I asked.

"Daniel. He's eleven, followed your whole career."

I uncapped the pen and scribbled a message before handing both of them to him. "Would you like to get a photo?"

"That would be... thank you," he stuttered, digging out his cell.

Felicity came around to us and took the phone. "Say Quakers."

I bit down on my cheek to stop chuckling.

"I took a couple." She handed him the phone.

"Thank you so much. My son will be so excited."

"You tell him to stay strong."

"I will, and thanks again." He sniffled, and I could see the flash of pain in his eyes.

Shit, was his son really sick?

Something twisted inside me.

"Wait," I exhaled. "Maybe I could try to organize tickets for you to bring him down to a game."

"You could?" The guy went slack jawed.

"Yeah." Grabbing another napkin, I asked for the pen

back and wrote down our PR's number. "Call this number tomorrow and they'll get you set up."

"That is... thank you. Thank you so much."

"Anytime."

"Enjoy the rest of your evening."

The guy walked away, looking back one last time. He waved the napkin and mouthed 'Thank you' again.

"Jason, that was—"

"Don't," I breathed. I didn't want tonight to be about football, but this was my life, and it would only get more intense as I progressed through college, moving ever closer to my NFL dream.

"Excuse me," I signaled to the server, "can we get the check please?"

Despite our private table in the corner of the room, other people had started to glance in our direction. If we didn't get out of here soon, there was every chance we'd never make it.

"I'm sorry." I ran a hand down my face. "I thought we'd have more privacy."

"This is your life, Jason, I understand." There was a flicker of sadness in her voice that damn near gutted me.

"But I don't just want it to be my life, babe. I want it to be *our* life. Look, I know things have been intense the last few weeks... but the team—"

"Are important, I get it. This is your dream. I knew what I was signing on for."

Except she didn't. No one truly could until they'd lived it.

"I guess I just feel like everyone has it all figured out.

You're doing amazing, and I'm so proud of you, Jason, I am. You manage the team, your classes. Hailee and Cameron are loving Michigan and have made a whole life for themselves. Asher and Mya are... well, they're Asher and Mya, nothing fazes them."

I didn't like hearing Felicity talk like that, as if everyone had found their place except her. Especially not when her place was right by my side.

"We should go..." She grabbed her purse.

"Talk to me, please. I don't want football to come between us, not tonight."

"It isn't just football, Jason, it's... everything."

Well, shit.

I'd known things were bad. But perhaps I'd underestimated how much.

"Look, let's go back to the apartment and talk. I hate that you're feeling like this."

"Okay." Felicity gave me a small nod.

I dug out my wallet and pulled out some bills, adding them to the check. "Come on." I reached for her hand. "Let's go home.

Felicity

The night had been perfect. The restaurant was romantic with its sultry mood lighting and incredible views. The food was to die for. And being with Jason away from all the pressure of classes and the team was heavenly.

Until the stranger had approached asking for an

autograph, and just like that the illusion came crumbling down around us, giving me a snapshot of what life with Jason would always be like. The more successful he became, the more recognized he became. The more recognized he became, the more the spotlight would shine down on him. And the more the spotlight shone, the more I wilted into the shadows.

"It's chilly," I said, as he held open the door for me and we spilled out into the inky night. Thanksgiving was in less than three weeks, and with it, the end of the football season.

Until next year.

"What are you—"

"Ford? What the hell, man," Griffin ambled over to us, a small group of people trailing behind. "Fancy running into you guys."

"Hey, Jason. We were just talking about you."

My spine bristled at Shelly Halstead's dulcet tone. She didn't even look twice at me, fixing her overly made up eyes right on Jason.

"All good, I hope?" He gave a strained laugh, clutching my hand tighter.

"Oh, you know it." She smirked, licking her lips seductively.

"We're meeting Gio and a few of the guys at The Gridiron. You and Fee should come, hang out."

"Actually, we're just on our way home," I said, giving Griffin a weak smile.

"Come on, one drink." He pouted.

"You should totally come, Jason." Shelly twirled a

strand of hair around her finger. She couldn't have been any more obvious if she'd tried.

But what did I expect?

Jason was the star... and I was invisible by all accounts.

"You should go," I said before I could stop myself.

He gave me a confused look.

"Go, hang out with your friends. I'll see you back at the apartment."

"What are—"

I took a step backward right as Griffin and Shelly grabbed Jason and started steering him in the opposite direction. "We'll return him to you in one piece," Griffin called, but I was already hurrying away from them.

Tears burned the backs of my eyes as I folded my arms around myself and tried to fight the wave of emotion crashing over me.

"Felicity, wait..."

His voice gave me pause but it only made me angrier. It was irrational, I knew that. But I also knew Shelly had completely dismissed me just now, as if I was no one. Insignificant. Just a bug to be stepped on.

"Felicity, will you just wait a second?" He snagged my arm and I finally stopped, inhaling a ragged breath. "What are you doing?"

I pressed my lips together, willing myself not to cry. But tears clung precariously to my lashes.

"Felicity, babe, look at me." Jason began to turn me in his arms. "What the fuck is going on?"

"She just acted like I wasn't even there." I could barely

look at him. This wasn't me. I wasn't insecure about a jersey chaser.

And yet...

"Shelly, you're worried about *Shelly*? She's no one to me, you know that."

"I know." My bottom lip quivered.

"Have I ever given you a reason to doubt me?"

I shook my head, unable to find the words to even begin to explain what was going on in my head, when I didn't even truly understand it myself.

"You know I wouldn't have gone with them just now, right?"

My eyes dropped, hating that such a lovely night was ruined.

"Look at me." Jason slid his fingers under my jaw and tilted my face. "I need to hear you say the words, Felicity."

"I know," I whispered.

"Good." His lips thinned. "Now can we please go home and salvage what was supposed to be a romantic night?"

"Okay," I said the words, but I didn't feel them. I was still stuck on that sidewalk, watching Shelly blatantly lust after my boyfriend as if I was nothing.

Wondering why it mattered so much.

Jason

Felicity was quiet the whole way home. Fucking Griffin and Shelly. It was as if the universe just wanted to fuck with me a little more, planting them right outside the restaurant. One minute we were all standing there, and the next, Felicity was telling me to go with them, as if I'd ever just abandon her like that.

Fuck. It stung.

By the time we made it up to our apartment, the air was thick and suffocating around us. I wanted to apologize, to spend the night showing her how much I loved her. How much I fucking needed her. But now... now I didn't know what to say, let alone know how we even got to this point.

The second she opened the door, Felicity took off into the apartment.

I snagged her wrist. "Wait, we need to talk."

"I'm tired, Jason. I think I'm just going to—"

"Fuck. That," I ground out, feeling the edges of my control fray.

She spun around to face me, her eyes holding so much defeat, I felt sucker punched. "I don't want to do this right now."

"Do what? You're talking like we're over or something."

Her eyes flickered to the ground. It was only a split second, but it was enough for my heart to plummet into my fucking toes.

She wanted to end it?

No.

No way.

It was just an argument. A silly argument after a few weeks of strain. It was nothing we couldn't fix. But then she said seven little words that made me stumble back.

"I'm not sure I can do this anymore."

"What?" I blinked at her. "What the fuck did you just say?"

We stared at each other for the longest second. Tears glossed Felicity's eyes, streaking down her cheeks.

"Hold up, this is all because Shelly was there?"

"She acted like I was no one, Jason. Do you have any idea how horrible that makes me feel? Knowing that she thinks she can have you? As if I'm nothing."

"Babe." I stepped forward, needing to touch her. Needing to stop any more ridiculous words coming out of her mouth. "You know what she's like." A lot of the cheerleaders were the same, all desperate to bag a player. And unfortunately for me, I was at the top of the food chain. But I'd never even looked, let alone touched.

Not when I had all I could want right here.

"I thought I was strong enough..." she murmured, dropping her gaze again. "I thought we would come here, and I'd be at your side..."

"You are at my side." I grabbed her shoulders. "You're the only one I need at my side. I know I've been prioritizing the team, but it's just for a few more weeks and then the season is over, and things will calm down." My eyes bored into hers, pleading with her to believe me. "Shit, babe, where is all this coming from?"

"I'm barely keeping my head above water, Jason. And you... you make it look so easy. You have friends, the team, an endless stream of girls vying for your attention. That guy tonight, at the restaurant, he's going to be the first of many. And I'm proud of you... God, I'm so proud of you. This is all you've ever wanted..."

My jaw clenched. The more she spoke, the more resigned she sounded. I gently laid my hand along the side of her neck. "I need you to hear what I'm about to say. You think I'm not blind with jealousy over the idea of you spending all your spare time with tutor boy? That it doesn't drive me crazy knowing you've found someone to connect with about the thing *you* love? I. Fucking. Hate. It." My fingers brushed her throat, feeling her pulse flutter beneath my fingers.

"I hate that you've found it hard to make friends and I hate how much I've let you down. But do you know what I hate the most? I hate that you're standing there, doubting that I want you." My hand dropped to the neckline of her sweater dress, gently tugging it down to reveal my brand on her skin. My thumb traced the small lettering. "What does it say?" I asked her.

"J- Jason."

"Tell me what it says."

"P- property of a Raider."

"Damn right it does. You're mine, Giles." My hand slid back to her neck, holding her gently as I stared right into her eyes. "None of this means anything if you're not by my side."

Her lip quivered as she bit back a fresh wave of tears.

"I love you, woman. I love you too fucking much to ever let you walk away from me."

"It's only going to get harder," she breathed. "Classes, your football career. What if I'm not strong—"

"Ssh." I slid my thumb over her lips, leaning down to touch my head to hers. "You're one of the strongest people I know, babe. Your heart, your compassion, the way you love so fiercely. I'm a lucky bastard to call you mine. I know things are hard right now, and I hate that I've made you doubt me, doubt us... but I need you, Felicity. I will always need you."

A whimper escaped her lips, but I swallowed it, sealing my mouth over hers, and kissing her with everything I felt. The good, the bad... the downright unthinkable. Losing Felicity was not an option.

Not today.

Not tomorrow.

Not ever.

I just needed to figure out a way to show her that.

7

Felicity

I could taste the salty wetness of my tears as Jason pushed his tongue into my mouth and kissed me. Only, he didn't just kiss me, he branded me. Marked me with his teeth and claimed me with his touch.

There were still things we needed to talk about, insecurities I needed to address, but for now, I allowed myself to get lost in the way he dominated my every thought.

"You look so fucking sexy in this dress." His hands slipped down the back of my thighs and he hoisted me against him, forcing my legs around his waist. I could already feel him hard at my stomach. Thick and ready. Desire pulsed through me like a heartbeat.

"Jason," I gasped, as he stalked me across the room and pushed me up against the wall.

Everything became desperate. We clawed at each other's clothes, skin, and muscle. My fingers raked across Jason's shoulders and back as he trailed hot wet kisses down my jaw and throat, lingering on my pulse point, flicking his tongue over my burning skin.

My hair cascaded around me as I dropped my head

against the wall, greedy for more. Jason walked his fingers down my stomach, finding the hem of my dress and pushing it up my body, before sliding his hand between us.

"Oh God," I cried as he rubbed me over my lace panties, creating an intoxicating friction.

"Fuck, babe, you're so wet." Hooking the material aside, he pushed two fingers inside me. A garbled moan broke from my lips as he added his thumb, dragging it over my clit. "This is mine," he uttered against the corner of my mouth. "Always." He curled his fingers, rubbing harder. "Forever." He nipped my bottom lip, soothing the sting with his tongue. "Mine."

A wave of intense pleasure crashed over me as I cried his name over and over. My hand went to his belt buckle, pulling it free and working his jeans off his hips just enough that his dick sprung free.

I needed him.

I needed him more than I had ever needed him before.

My hunger was frenzied, coursing inside me like wildfire. Jason's eyes locked on mine as he slowly rocked forward, filling me to the hilt. "Fuck," he breathed.

"Move," I begged, my voice thick with lust. "I need you to—" The air *whooshed* from my lungs as he pulled out and slammed back inside of me.

He wasn't gentle or tender, slow or sweet. Jason wasn't making love to me now, he was imprinting himself on my soul, trying to carve his name on my bones.

"Mine," he growled against my ear before running his tongue down my neck, licking and sucking.

"Jason, I can't... it's—"

"Ssh." He pressed his head against mine, pinning me to the wall with his intense gaze. "I know what you need, Felicity. I will always know." He punched his hips forward making us both cry out in ecstasy.

My hands wound around his neck, holding on for dear life. I would ache tomorrow, the wall rough against my back, my thighs pressed wide to accommodate Jason's big body.

But right there, in that moment, I didn't care. Because we were just two people so desperately and irrevocably in love that we were drowning in each other.

And I didn't ever want to come up for air.

Jason

I told Coach I was going to be late to morning conditioning. After last night, I didn't want to just up and leave this morning. I meant everything I'd said, but I wasn't dipshit enough not to know that it wasn't about what *I said*, it was about how *Felicity felt*.

I watched her sleep for a while. The soft rise and fall of her chest, the slight scrunch to her nose as she dreamed—of me hopefully—and the way her perfect fucking tits jiggled with every breath.

Felicity was all I ever wanted. Every part of me was tied to every part of her, so the fact she doubted this, doubted us, it fucking killed me.

I'd tried to show her last night, but I knew sex wasn't the answer.

But fuck, if it hadn't blown my mind all the same. It felt

like forever since I'd taken her so urgently. I hadn't wanted to stop, high on the feel of her thighs pulling me closer, her perfect body pinned against the wall, on display for me. Her tattoo taunting me while I rocked into her over and over.

I reached out, tracing the curve of her hip where the sheet had fallen down her body.

"Jason," she murmured.

"It's me. Go back to sleep."

"You're still here?"

"I told Coach I'd be late." I shuffled down the bed, pressing my body against the soft curves of hers.

"You did?" She finally cracked an eye open.

"Yeah. After last night..."

"Ssh." Her finger pressed against my lips, the way mine had hers last night. "I don't want to talk; I just want to enjoy this."

Pushing the hair from Felicity's face, I brushed my nose over hers. "I love you. You know that, right?"

"I know." Her hand splayed over my chest, right where my heart lay. "I love you too."

My shoulders sagged with relief. I hadn't realized how much I needed to hear those words until now. "We'll get through this, I promise." Because anything else was not an option.

Felicity nodded. "What time do you have to leave?"

"I still have an hour."

"Better make the most of it then." She reached down and grasped my morning wood, sending a bolt of pleasure up my spine.

"Actually," I couldn't believe I was doing this, "I was hoping to take you to breakfast." I kissed the end of her nose.

"Yeah?" Her uncertain smile made my heart crack wide open.

Damn, I had some making up to do. But I didn't want to rush headfirst into shallow apologies and hasty grand declarations of love.

I wanted to show her, without doubt, that she was it for me.

But first, I wanted to take my girl to breakfast and feed her.

———

"Good?" I asked, watching with rapt fascination, and a touch of jealousy, as Felicity devoured her blueberry muffin.

"So good." She grinned.

Mr. Java's was a coffee shop off campus. It was less crowded, and we'd been able to grab a table by the window.

"So did Mya mention the Thanksgiving thing Asher's mom is throwing?"

"Yeah."

"And?"

"I assumed we'd go." Felicity smiled. "She said I can invite my parents, or I'll see them before."

Things with Felicity's dad were still strained. He didn't

look at me like I'd stolen and corrupted his only daughter anymore, but he still wasn't my biggest fan either.

"Then we'll all come back here on Friday to watch the game."

Fuck.

The final game.

The season close was fast approaching.

"Asher also mentioned the possibility of spending a weekend in New York after the season is over. It could be pretty romantic."

"That sounds nice." Felicity smiled but it didn't reach her eyes.

"Babe, me and you, we're—"

"Hey, I didn't expect to see you here." Tutor boy loomed down over us, setting my jaw on edge.

"Oh, hey, Darcy. You remember my boyfriend, Jason?"

"As if I could forget. You're big news around campus."

"We've had a good season so far." I sat back in my chair, dragging one leg over my knee. Darcy was a preppy type. Slacks and a sweater, hair slicked back, and a messenger bag looped over his shoulder. He was everything I wasn't, everything I didn't want to be. Yet, I couldn't help but wonder if Felicity ever wished she'd fallen for someone more like him.

What the fuck was I doing?

Felicity didn't want someone like Darcy Bannerman. She needed someone to temper her wild spirit, put up with her special brand of crazy.

She needed me.

"We all set for our session later?" He ignored my eyes drilling into his head and focused solely on my girl.

I had the sudden need to claim her, right there in the middle of the fucking coffee shop. I shifted uncomfortably, pissed that he was invoking such a carnal reaction from me.

Now you know how Felicity feels, asshole.

"Yeah, I'll see you later, okay?" Her polite dismissal made my heart soar.

"Uh, sure." Tutor boy hesitated. "I'll see you later. Jason, it was a pleasure."

I bet it was, asshole.

He left the coffee shop and Felicity let out a little sigh of relief. "You can stop glaring now." She chuckled.

"Do you ever wish—"

"Don't even say it. I don't want Darcy, he's my tutor."

"Yeah, but he gets all that stuff you love so much."

God, why was everything so fucking messed up? It was like we took one step forward and two steps back.

"Jason, I love you." Felicity shuffled forward on her chair. "I guess I just underestimated how hard all this would be."

"I know and I wish it could be different. But—"

"I get it, I do. I would never ever want you to give up your dream. You've worked too hard for it."

"I love you."

The words were fast becoming a stitch for the frayed seams of our relationship. But I didn't know how to fix it. I didn't know how to make Felicity believe I needed her.

Her green eyes fluttered closed and when she opened

them again, all I saw was a girl desperately trying to cling onto her dream.

She gave me a sad smile and said, "I know."

Felicity

"Hello, do you mind if I sit here?" I said to the girl meticulously unpacking her supplies onto the small desk.

"Sure." She barely glanced at me.

After breakfast with Jason on Monday, I'd decided to brush myself off and revert back to my old habit of making a list. Back in high school, it had helped me feel in control of my life, so why not here?

But instead of writing a college bucket list, I'd decided to keep it simple. One task a day.

Today's task: make a new friend.

It sounded simple, and yet, it was something I'd struggled with. Even in my classes full of likeminded students, I'd failed to really connect with anyone. But I'd noticed Elodie and she was always alone, always sitting at the back of lectures. So I'd decided that maybe she was like me; maybe she also found it hard to connect.

"I'm Felicity," I said. "Felicity Giles."

"Oh. My. God," she breathed. "I thought it was you." Her whole face transformed. Gone was the shy, quiet student I'd seen around classes, replaced with a starry-eyed girl who stared at me like I was the second coming.

"I mean, I've heard your name around... but I didn't know... wow. You're like dating Jason Ford. That is... wow. I'm a huge fan."

My lips pressed into a thin line. I couldn't escape. No matter where I turned, who I talked to, I would always be *Jason Ford's girlfriend*.

"That's me." I gave her a weak smile. I didn't have the heart to ruin her morning since she seemed so excited to be talking to me.

"I'm a huge fan... huge. Followed the Quakers my whole life. My dad played for them... he's kind of Quaker royalty. That's why I keep myself to myself." She glanced around conspiratorially. "And oh my god, I'm doing it, aren't I? I'm totally being that weird obsessed fan that I try so hard to avoid."

"Yeah, you kind of are." Strangled laughter bubbled in my chest.

"I'm sorry, it's just... damn, girl." She clutched the edge of her desk and leaned closer. "You're dating *Jason Ford*, one of the best quarterbacks the NCAA has seen in at least a decade. That's got to be something."

Oh, it was something all right.

"Hey, would you like to get a coffee after class? In a totally non-creeper kind of way. I'm Elodie by the way. Elodie Faltham."

"I..."

This so wasn't how I'd seen the conversation going. I'd wanted to make a friend, to strike up conversation with someone who wouldn't automatically pigeonhole me as Jason Ford's girlfriend. But maybe she got it, maybe she understood more than most.

"I promise I'm not usually this weird," she added as if she could hear my inner turmoil. "I'm just passionate about the things I love, and it just so happens I really love football, almost as much as I love animals." Her smile grew.

That sealed the deal.

A girl who could love football *and* animals...

Despite her shaky introduction, Elodie Faltham sounded like my kind of girl.

8

Felicity

"Holy freaking crap, this is amazing," Elodie shrieked beside me as the team jogged out onto the field.

Jordan had needed to go home for the weekend, something to do with a family emergency. She kindly offered to donate her ticket to my *new friend*. I wasn't sure Elodie warranted friend status yet, but we had hung out a couple of times, and we always sat together in class now. After her initial excitement that I was dating Jason, she reined herself in, and kept our conversation to safer topics like my volunteer work at the shelter and her dream of one day working with big cats in African reservations.

"I mean, I've been to all their games, but I've never even come close to scoring seats this good. Thank you so much." She gave me a big grin and I couldn't help but be infected by her enthusiasm. She reminded me of... well, me back in high school, eager to soak up senior year and all that came with it.

"Oh my god, there he is." She pointed to Jason and I let out a small chuckle.

"Yep, that's him."

"Oh God, I'm doing it again, aren't I?" Her brows knitted. "I'm sorry, it's just—"

"It's okay. Enjoy it."

The atmosphere in Franklin Field was electric, everyone high on the team's perfect season so far. If they won tonight, it would leave them with two games to play and the league title in sight.

I knew how much it meant to the team, the fans, and the coaches. But most of all, I knew how much it meant to the guy wearing the red and blue number one jersey.

"If they win this game, the season could be theirs. Only Dartmouth has a shot at taking it from..." She launched into an analysis of the Ivy League, but her words barely registered as I watched Jason command his teammates. They respected him, followed his orders, and paid attention when he talked. It was something to behold.

We were in a better place since the weekend. There were still some things we needed to work through, but something had shifted.

"Felicity?" Elodie nudged me.

"Huh, sorry?"

"I said are you sure about me coming to the party later? I've never been to a football party before."

"It's just like any other college party really, except with more cheerleaders."

"Actually," her cheeks pinked, "I've never really been to a college party before."

"I've probably been to less than you can imagine," I admitted.

"What, no way? Your boyfriend is—"

"I think we've established who my boyfriend is." I gave her an amused smile. "But I haven't exactly spread my wings since coming to Penn."

"Well, we can be out of our comfort zone together." Elodie shot me a conspiratorial wink.

"Aren't you worried about people finding out about your dad?"

She shrugged. "Honestly, I think I've been using him as a reason not to push myself into new social situations."

"So tonight, we party?" A trickle of excitement zipped through me. I'd always gone to parties with Jason, stood and watched from the sidelines as he and his friends let loose and enjoyed themselves. Jordan had been around this semester, but last year it had mostly been me. So I couldn't deny it felt nice to finally have someone in my corner.

Even if she was infatuated with my boyfriend.

Jason

"Congratulations." Felicity rushed over to me as I found her in the lingering crowd.

I pulled her into my arms and kissed her. Adrenaline still pumped through my veins, a firestorm showing no signs of letting up. I either needed a strong drink or to be buried deep inside my girl. But there was a party... a party I'd promised the guys I would make an appearance at.

Fuck.

"I'm so proud of you."

We'd beat Yale 28-17. We were unstoppable, a

relentless storm determined to blow right through every team we came up against. And next on the list was Cornell.

My eyes went over Felicity's shoulder when I realized we had company. "You must be Elodie," I said, pulling Felicity into my side. "I'm Jason."

The girl's eyes went wide, her mouth hanging open.

"El, we talked about this," Felicity said as if they were old friends. I'd heard all about Elodie Faltham, daughter of Quaker legend Marcus Faltham, star running back in the late eighties. She was Felicity's new friend. Although I was beginning to think there was something wrong with her with the way she was gawking.

"H- hi, it's an honor." She held out her hand, and I stared at it, frowning. "Oh, right, sorry." She jammed it into her pocket. "I'm not usually this nervous. It's just I'm a huge fan."

"Guess it runs in the family, huh?"

"Yeah." She gulped. "My dad started me young."

"I know that feeling," I grumbled. "Are you ready to party with the team?"

"I..." She rolled her lips together, but I could see she was almost ready to burst with excitement.

"She's a little excited."

"The team is going to love having Quaker royalty in the house."

"Oh no, you can't tell them, please?" Her whole demeanor changed.

"Sure, yeah, okay." I glanced at Felicity and she gave me an imperceptible shake of her head.

Just what I needed. A party I didn't want to go to, a

girlfriend who was questioning our relationship at every turn, and a fan who looked like she'd never partied in her life.

Tonight, was going to be a fucking disaster.

———

The party was already in full swing by the time we arrived. Felicity wanted to run by the apartment and change. She'd let Elodie borrow an outfit and the two of them looked dressed to kill. It didn't worry me where Felicity was concerned—everyone knew she was off limits. But Elodie was fresh meat and so far out of her comfort zone she may as well have worn a neon sign.

"Oh wow, that's a lot of people," she breathed, her eyes wide with wonder as she took in the house.

"Don't worry," Felicity squeezed her hand, "we'll get a couple of drinks inside you and you'll be fine."

"I'm sure Griffin or one of the guys will be more than happy to help—"

"*Jason.*"

"What?" I balked. If Felicity thought I was going to spend the night playing babysitter, she was sorely mistaken. I wanted to show my face, have a couple of beers, and then get the hell out of there.

"We can't just let the guys loose on her."

"Relax, I'm joking." Mostly. But Elodie was already gone, walking into the house as if she was entering a magical wonderland or some shit.

I hooked an arm around Felicity and dragged her into

my side. She pressed a hand against my chest, gazing up at me. "Are you okay being here?"

"I am." She nodded. "Who knows, maybe I'll even have some fun?" Her eyes flicked to Elodie.

My brows knitted together. "Are you saying you don't have fun with me?"

"You know what I mean." She leaned up to kiss me, scraping her nails lightly over my jaw. Blood flowed straight to my dick and I groaned under my breath when she grabbed my hand and yanked me into the house.

"Yo, Ford, get over here."

Music pumped out of a speaker somewhere, bodies already grinding and rubbing on each other. Griffin and Gio made a beeline for me, pulling me into a guy hug. I tried to keep hold of Felicity's hand, but she let me go, mouthing, "I'm going to find Elodie," who had already disappeared into the sea of people.

"Behave," I yelled, because although we were in a house full of teammates, Felicity was still my girl.

And I really didn't want to spend the night fighting off the vultures.

Felicity

"I think I'm drunk," Elodie giggled, burying her face in Griffin's shoulder.

"How many did she have?" he asked me, and I shrugged.

"About four." As opposed to my eight, but even after

double the amount of drinks, I still wasn't as drunk as my new friend.

"Four? Holy shit, she's—"

"Happy." Her head snapped up. "I'm sooo happy. Let's do more of those funky smelling shots." She started to reach for the rest beside her six-foot two leaning post, but Griffin wrapped her into a bear hug. "Oh no you don't, new girl."

"I'll have one," I piped up.

"I think you've had enough," Jason ground out.

"Oh, don't be such a spoilsport." I tapped his cheek. "We're having fun."

"Fun." Elodie punched the air, almost falling backward but Griffin steadied her. He seemed smitten, a glint in his eye.

"You need to watch Griff," I whispered to Jason, swaying gently. "He's looking at El the way you look at me."

"Oh yeah?" He dipped his head to mine, electricity crackling between us. "And how do I look at you?"

"Like you want to devour me."

Jason smirked, stealing a chaste kiss. "You're fun when you're drunk."

"Then I should probably drink more." I shot him a saucy wink before diving for the tray of shooters.

I don't know what came over me, but for the first time in a long time, I felt like my old self. Fun and free and not tied down by the weight of expectation and responsibility. It was ironic really, but it seemed that the quiet, shy girl from my class had unleashed something inside me.

I downed the murky looking drink and wiped my

mouth with the back of my hand, enjoying the burn as it slid down my throat.

"Your girl is on form tonight, Ford." Griffin said, his arm still wrapped around Elodie.

"Fee is the best," she slurred. "I think I have a girl crush."

"Okay, drunk girl." I wrangled her off Griffin. "We are going to dance."

"Dance?" She shrieked. "But I don't dance."

"Well," I grinned, "you do now."

———

The room was spinning. Sweat coated my skin, little beads of moisture trailing down my back and chest as we moved to the beat. I'd lost track of time, dancing and laughing. No one bothered us, not with Jase and Griffin standing watch like two sentries put on the Earth with the sole purpose of protecting us.

"I think Griff likes you," I said to my new friend. She'd switched to water earlier, protesting when Griffin had insisted she drink it. But I knew she'd thank him tomorrow morning when she woke. Although I had a sneaky suspicion she wouldn't be waking up in her own bed.

"I don't feel so good," I reached out for her, a wave of nausea crashing over me.

"Shit, Felicity—"

Strong arms caught me. "I'm taking you home."

"But I'm still dancing." I stared up at my savior.

"Babe, you can barely stand." Jason pulled me into his

side and said something to Elodie and Griffin. Over the music and the blood pounding between my ears, I could barely make out a single word.

Then we were moving. Cool air rushing over my skin and dousing the heat coursing through my veins. "Wait." I sagged against Jason's body. "I don't feel so good."

"I got you, babe," he said, sounding far too sober. Come to think of it, I hadn't seen him with a drink for hours.

"Why aren't you drunk?" The words came out a garbled mess as he propped me against the wall so I could catch my breath.

"I had two beers then switched to soda."

"But why? It's a celebration... everyone came to celebrate you." All night I'd watched people gravitate to Jason. He was the sun and they wanted to be in his orbit.

Or was it gravity?

Huh.

"I wanted you to enjoy yourself."

"But you could have relaxed too."

"I think you underestimate the level I will go to protect you." He kissed the end of my nose. "How are you feeling now?"

"Okay, I think. Your swoony words sobered me a little." A smile tugged at my lips.

"One-hundred percent truth, babe."

"God, I love you. I love you so much I wish this didn't ever have to end." A rush of love swelled inside me, like rising waters threatening to pull me under.

"Good thing it doesn't ever have to end then. Come on." He started to pull me along with him.

"It will though. One day you'll be super famous, and I'll be a college dropout. I'll still love you then, you know... even when you're a hotshot in the NFL and I have to get my glimpses of you on ESPN."

"You're drunk, babe."

"That may be so, but I'm also a realist... and this... us... it isn't endgame. It's—" My ankle rolled, and the world began to fall away.

"Shit, Felicity."

"I'm flyiiiiing." I chuckled, throwing my arms out to the side and bracing myself for impact.

But it never came.

"You caught me," I said, staring up at intense dark eyes I didn't think I would ever forget. Because those eyes were my world. Everything I ever wanted.

"I will always catch you, Giles."

God, how I wanted to believe him.

9

Jason

"This is it, ladies. Win tonight and the title is ours." Coach leveled us with a hard look.

Our win against Cornell last week meant we could be crowned league winners tonight, instead of our last game. And the best fucking part? Cam and Asher were in the crowd, thanks to their teams having bye weeks.

"I couldn't have asked for more from you this season," he went on. "Losing Lincoln was a blow, but, Jason, son, you rose to the challenge and got the job done."

Everyone cheered, the stamp of their cleats against the floor and the shrill of their hollers rattling inside my chest.

"It's so close we can almost taste it. Penn hasn't had a season like this in almost a decade. Go out there and do what you were born to do. Now everyone get in here."

We rose like an army answering a battle cry and wedged around Coach in a circle. "Quakers on three." He gave me the nod and my voice pierced the air.

"One... two... three... Quakers."

Gio clapped me on the back, his eyes dancing with anticipation. "Yo, Griff, is your girl gonna be out there?"

"Fuck off, she's not my girl."

"Not what I heard," I added around a smirk.

Since the party, Felicity and Elodie had hung out a lot. She'd even talked me into going on a couple of double dates with Griff and her new friend. He didn't want to put a label on it, but the two of them seemed close. I'd seen the protective glint in his eye that night. He barely let her out of his sight. Elodie was a strange one. At times, she was desperately quiet and introverted, and then other times she was vibrant and talked at a mile a minute. But Felicity liked her. And there wasn't much I wouldn't do for that girl.

As we grabbed our helmets and filed out of the locker room, my mind went to that night again. Felicity had been ass over elbow drunk, spewing all kinds of shit about us, about me. Things I didn't ever want to hear. But when she'd woken up the next morning, hungover and dehydrated, I hadn't had the heart to bring it up with her. So we'd danced around it. If she remembered, she never said anything, and I tried every day to reassure her that I loved her.

To reassure her that her fears were never going to manifest into reality.

Things were better... but they weren't perfect. She was still hanging around with tutor boy and I was still with the team more often than not.

Hopefully though, after tonight that would all change.

"You ready for this?" Gio shoulder-checked me as we spilled onto the field. It was a blessing to have our penultimate game at home. If we won tonight, the atmosphere in Franklin Field would be explosive, and the hunger for it burned in my veins.

"Born ready," I muttered, letting the crowd's cheers wash over me. Felicity was the girl for me. I felt it in my soul as sure as I knew the sky was blue and the grass beneath my feet was green. One day, I would put a ring on her finger and my kid in her stomach. She was my heart. But football? Football was my calling.

I just had to find a way to make the two symbiotic.

A big hand landed on my shoulder and I looked up to find Griff staring at me. "I finally get it," he mumbled.

"Yeah, and what's that?" I teased.

"I like her, man. I really fucking like her."

My lips curved. "Well hold that thought, because we have a game to win." I clapped him on the back and started jogging toward the rest of our team.

"How'd you do it?" he called.

I spun around, jogging backward. "Do what?"

"Focus on football *and* a girl?"

"You just gotta show her what she means to you."

The words were like a punch to the stomach. My step faltered as every memory Felicity and I shared slammed into me one after another.

Everything was so clear... I didn't know how I hadn't seen it before.

I knew what I had to do.

I knew how to fix us.

Felicity

Tears streamed down my face as I watched Jason and his teammates celebrate. The thirteen-thousand strong crowd was on their feet, clapping and cheering, celebrating right along with them.

I watched with nothing but pride and love as Coach Faulkner found Jason and pulled him into a hug before holding his shoulders and saying something to him. Jason nodded, his eyes wide with understanding.

"Your boy did good." Hailee nestled into my side, her own pride and excitement swirling around us. This moment didn't only mean a lot to me, it meant a lot to all of us. Cam, Asher, Hailee, even Mya. We knew what football meant to Jason, what *this moment* would mean for him.

I dabbed my eyes, trying to get a hold of my emotions. Being here to witness this, seeing the guy I loved more than anything make his dreams come true... well, it was easy to forget all the strain and distance between us over the last few weeks. My heart swelled for him. The boy from Rixon with a dream of making it. A boy who had stolen my heart and refused to let it go.

He wanted football *and* me.

If only it were that simple.

"Flick, you should go down there," Asher said, nudging me from behind.

"What? I can't just—"

"He's looking for you."

Sure enough, Jason was searching the crowd for me. We hadn't been able to sit in the VIP section since there was six of us, so I'd given Elodie my ticket and she and Jordan were down there, while I sat in the bleachers with my friends.

The second Jason's eyes found mine, everything melted away. On shaky legs, I hurried down the steps to the barrier. Jason jogged toward me, his smile radiant and eyes filled with sweet relief.

"You did it," I breathed, pressing my palms against his shoulders. His hair was damp and messy, his Quaker jersey streaked with mud and grass stains as his helmet hung at his side.

"I can't..." He swallowed roughly. "This is... I can't believe it."

"Believe it, Jason." One of my hands slid to his cheek. No matter what happened between us, wherever our road led, I would always want this for him. Even if it became the thing that ultimately destroyed us, Jason deserved this.

He deserved his dreams to come true.

"I am so proud of you." I leaned down to kiss him, and a chorus of cheers broke out behind us. My cheeks pinked and I tried to pull away, but Jason slid one of his hands around the back of my neck, anchoring me in place. "Babe, I couldn't have done it without you," he whispered against my lips. "I need you, Felicity Charlotte Giles. I will always need you."

I opened my mouth to reply, but the guys charged at him, yanking him backwards.

"Sorry, Fee," Griff yelled. "But we need to borrow our fearless leader."

Laughter escaped my lips as I watched them.

Part of me wanted to hate the very thing that might one day take Jason from me, but right there, in that moment, I could only feel joy.

Jason

We didn't stay and party with the team. Despite their protests, after a couple of drinks, a lot of high fives and congratulations, I wanted nothing more than to celebrate with my friends and my girl, so we left.

"Shit, man, that was really something." Asher clinked his beer against mine as we sat huddled in a quiet booth toward the back of the bar underneath Asher and Mya's building. I hadn't wanted to be accosted by adoring fans, not tonight.

"You know, after that performance, teams will be lining up for you?"

"Don't speak so soon, there's still another two years left." And after Linc, we all knew how quickly your dream could go up in flames. His surgery had gone well, but his rehab would take a while. *If* he played again, there was every chance he wouldn't be the same player.

Asher snorted. "We'll see. Come graduation, you'll be signed with the Eagles or the Steelers, I'll be ready to start up a new branch of my old man's business, and fuck knows what this one will be doing."

"Hey." Cam punched his arm. "I have plans."

"Care to share then? Because I don't think I've ever heard you talk about what happens after graduation. In fact, I wouldn't put it past you to have a ring on her finger and a kid on the way." Asher smirked.

"Who's got a kid on the way?" Mya and the girls approached, frowning at the three of us.

"Umm, no one." He hooked an arm around her waist and pulled her down beside him.

I got up to let Hailee squeeze in between me and Cam, before pulling Felicity down on my knee. Scooping her hair out of the way, I nuzzled her neck. She leaned back, wrapping her arm around my neck. "Tired?" she asked.

"I'm okay." I breathed her in before kissing her soft skin. A shiver ran through her body, igniting the fire in my veins.

"Don't mind us," Asher grumbled.

"Like you aren't a total horn dog after a game." Mya rolled her eyes and we all burst into laughter. It felt good.

It felt fucking amazing sitting there with my girl and my best friends in the whole world.

"So the Heisman—" Asher started, but I silenced him with a dark look.

"Heisman? What's he talking about?" Felicity glanced back at me.

"Ash seems to think Jason stands a good chance of being nominated," Cam answered her.

She twisted around to look at me. "Well, do you?"

I shrugged. "I doubt it. The Ivy League is usually overlooked."

"But there's a chance?" Hailee asked, and I met my stepsister's inquisitive gaze with a small nod.

"I guess."

"Holy shit, Jase, that's huge."

"The announcements aren't until early December, but seriously, you guys, don't get your hopes up. I'm not." I grabbed my beer and took a long pull. Felicity threaded our fingers together, her touch like a balm to my bruised and battered body. The game had been a dog fight. Brutal and relentless. But in the end, we had come out on top.

"Well, either way, my dad reserved the penthouse. It's ours for the entire weekend."

"We already booked our flights," Cam said.

"And I thought we could ride together?" Asher eyed me.

"Yeah, sure." I leaned back against the leather booth.

"You just won the Ivy League. You could try to seem a little more... I don't know, hyped."

"I'm hyped," I grunted. "It's just all on the inside."

The girls snickered. My arm snaked tighter around Felicity's waist and I let out a weary sigh. I was crashing, and I wanted nothing more than to go home, get naked, and fall to sleep wrapped in her arms.

Usually after a game, the adrenaline lingered. The high of the win or low of a defeat pulsing through my veins like a synthetic drug. But we'd done it. We'd won the title with a near perfect season. All the pressure had melted away, and I could finally relax.

I'd really done it.

"One more drink and then I think we'll head out," Felicity said, as if she had a direct line to my thoughts.

I fucking hoped she didn't.

Because there were things she didn't know yet.

Decisions I'd made that would affect us both.

"We can stay," I said. There was no pressure here. No guys chanting my name or fans wanting autographs. These guys knew me well enough to keep me grounded, to give me space.

And I fucking loved them for it.

10

Felicity

"So, you and Griff?" I waggled my brows at Elodie across the table.

"Are just friends." She pursed her lips, pretending to finish up the notes she was making.

"Friends who spend almost every night together?" My brow arched.

"Griff is..." She let out a long breath, tapping her pen against her lip. "He's complicated."

"Aren't they all? But the season is over now." The Quakers had ended with a perfect season, only making their title win all the sweeter.

"I'm happy to see where it goes, but I'm not under any illusion it's the real deal. Besides, Griff is a jock, his eyes will wander eventually." My stomach twisted and she paled. "Oh shit, Fee, I didn't mean..."

"I know." I did. She was firmly in the Jason/Felicity fan club.

"You guys are okay, right? Things seem... good."

"We're fine."

Elodie smiled. "And you have your weekend away to

look forward to. New York in December will be so romantic." She let out a dreamy sigh.

"Yeah, it will be nice." I was looking forward to seeing Hailee and Mya and spending some quality time with them without the pressure of classes. "I can't believe the semester is almost over."

"And we survived."

"We did," I said around a smile. I didn't doubt that my sessions with Darcy had a lot to do with my improved grades, but I was still relieved. I only had a couple more papers to submit before I was officially done for the holidays.

"Is that the time?" Elodie frowned. "I need to go." She collected up her things and stuffed them in her bag.

"Hot date?" I snickered.

"Griffin is taking me to The Gridiron for burgers."

"Romantic."

"We can't all be you, jetting off to New York for a weekend of romance." She stuck out her tongue before moving for the door.

"Hey, Elodie," I said as she grabbed the handle.

"Yeah?"

"I'm really glad I talked to you that day in class."

"Yeah." She beamed. "Me too."

Elodie left and I got comfy on the sofa. Grabbing my cell phone, I noticed I had a new text from Jason.

QB#1: Need to talk... are you home?

. . .

Me: Yeah. Elodie just left. Is everything okay?

QB#1: I'll be home soon.

My brows pinched. If Jason wanted to make me worry, he'd done a pretty good job of it. By the time I heard his key rattle in the door, I had a giant pit in my stomach.

Sitting forward, I waited for him to enter the apartment. "Hey." I searched his face for any sign of what was wrong, but he wore a mask of indifference.

"Hey," he said weakly, dropping down on the couch. Before I could ask what was wrong, Jason pulled me into his arms, burying his face in my shoulder.

"Jason, what is it? What's wrong?" Dread snaked through me.

His body trembled beneath my fingers as I held onto him as tight as he held me. Nudging him away with my shoulder, he finally straightened to look at me. "Coach called me."

"He did?"

"I'm in, babe... I made the final four."

"The Heisman Trophy?" My eyes grew to saucers. "Oh my god, Jason, that's amazing."

"I think I'm in shock." Another shudder rolled through him.

"Hey." I cupped his face. "You deserve this; you deserve it so much. Oh my god, your dad is going to freak."

"I already called him. He got all choked up."

"Well, yeah he did." I smiled. No one wanted this more for Jason than Kent Ford. "I thought you were coming here to tell me something bad."

"What?" Jason's brows furrowed. "What would I be—" his expression fell. "Us. You thought I was coming to talk about us."

"Honestly, I don't know what I thought, but you were so certain you wouldn't make the final cut."

"Come here, woman." He anchored his hand at the nape of my neck and guided my face to his. "What do I have to do to show you that me and you... we're endgame?"

"Jason..." I averted my gaze to escape his intense stare.

"No, babe. You need to hear me when I say it's you." He forced me to look at him. "It's always going to be you."

"I love you, Jason," I said, because it was true. It would always be true.

No matter where the future took us, my heart would always belong to Jason Ford.

Jason

"Good evening and thank you for joining us. Without you, the fans, college football and the Heisman Trophy would not be what they are today. I'm honored to be here this evening, representing the Heisman Trophy Trust. Congratulations to this year's finalists for their incredible feats on the field this college football season. We have so enjoyed watching you and following you in this year's Heisman race..."

The Heisman Trophy Trustee's voice was drowned out

by the blood roaring between my ears as I sat beside the other three finalists. My heart was beating like a bass drum in my chest, my palms were slick, and sweat beaded across my brow under the glare of the lights as the Trustee continued her speech.

"And now it's time to welcome a new member into our Heisman family. It is my pleasure to announce this year's winner..."

Time slowed down. I never expected to be here tonight. I never expected to be announced as a finalist... but now I was here, now it was a possibility, I wanted it.

I wanted it so fucking much.

"Jason Ford, University of Pennsylvania."

Cheers erupted behind me as I stood and shook hands with the other finalists, hardly able to believe my ears.

I'd won.

I'd fucking *won*.

"Congratulations, man," one of them said, but it all became white noise to the thrum of my heart in my chest.

This was... I had no fucking words.

Nothing.

It was a good thing Cameron and Asher had helped me write an acceptance speech just in case... because, fuck.

I moved toward the aisle behind me and my dad grabbed me, pulling me into a bear hug. "I'm so proud of you, son. So fucking proud."

"Thanks, Dad," I managed to choke out over the giant lump caught in my throat.

Denise was next, her overpowering perfume making

me cough as she enveloped me into a hug. "Congratulations, Jason. I know what this means to you."

We'd had a tenuous relationship when she and Hailee first moved in with me and my old man. Right up until senior year, I'd wanted nothing to do with her or her daughter. But as I moved along the line to my stepsister, I could no longer imagine not having her in my life.

"I'm so proud of you." Hailee hugged me, and I let her. Because I was no longer that same boy who had tormented her, and she was no longer the girl who rubbed me the wrong way.

"Get over here, bro." Cameron and Asher pulled me into a big group hug. The three of us silent as we acknowledged this moment.

The two of them had been there for every high, every low. They had seen me at my best, my worst, and every shade in between. And their loyalty and friendship had never faltered, not once.

Before I broke away, Ash grabbed my neck and pulled me close, "Now you go up there and own it, you hear me?" He shot me a wink, stepping aside to let me kiss Mya's cheek.

"Go get her, tiger," she whispered.

Felicity was waiting on the end, tears brimming in her eyes as she watched me close the distance between us. She looked stunning in the jade-green dress that fell over her curves like a silk waterfall.

"You did it," she breathed as I hauled her against my body, not caring we were in a room full of people, live on national television.

"I couldn't have done it without you." I couldn't explain it to her, but Felicity grounded me in a way that no other could. Her wild spirit and empathy, her passion and insecurities, everything about her anchored me. I needed that.

I needed it more than I'd ever realized.

"Go," she nodded to the stage, "they're waiting."

Stealing a kiss that barely touched my bone-deep need for her, I looped back around to the other row of chairs to shake hands with my coaches.

"Never doubted you for a second, son," Coach Faulkner said, giving me a rare smile.

"Thanks, Coach."

"Now get up there and do Penn proud."

With a swift nod, I made my way to the stage. "Congratulations, Jason." Someone guided me to the podium where the trophy was situated. I curled my hands over the bronze sculpture and lifted it in the air to hair-raising applause.

My heart beat so hard I felt a little lightheaded, but I couldn't wimp out now. This meant everything... *everything* to me. Placing the trophy back on its stand, I pulled the scrap of paper out of my pocket and looked out over the crowd.

"This is... wow. I should warn you now, I perform much better on the field." Emotion welled up inside me and I inhaled a shuddering breath, but the gentle laughs from the crowd settled my nerves. "I want to thank my team first. At the beginning of the season we lost our captain, Lincoln Manella, and Coach Faulkner asked me to step up as captain."

"Hell yeah, he did," Asher yelled, and everyone chuckled again.

"The team didn't only accept my leadership, they respected it. My O line: Gio, Klein, Macca, Treyvon, Austin, Louis, Paulie. Those guys have been unbelievable this season and I couldn't have done it without them. All my teammates have supported me and made this possible. I want to thank my coaches for guiding me right and keeping me grounded. For imparting their knowledge and pushing me to work harder." I gave an appreciative nod in the direction of Coach Faulkner and his team.

"I want to thank the team at Heisman for everything this weekend. For allowing me and my family to be here. It's an honor to stand on the same stage with some of my childhood idols." I glanced at the line of previous winners standing tall, all here to celebrate this moment. "I want to thank my dad, for pushing me to go harder, faster... for showing me what it takes to be the best. To my stepmom and sister, for being here today despite our history. My friends, my brothers in all the ways that matter, for always having my back. I'm so grateful. To the other finalists here tonight, it has been an incredible experience sharing our journeys and being in the company of such talent."

Taking another deep breath, I steeled my spine. "Earlier in the season, someone suggested that I could be in the running for the Heisman Trophy, but I dismissed it. No way a kid out of a small town in Pennsylvania, playing for an Ivy League team, was going to end up here tonight. But here I am." Another round of applause washed over me and I soaked it up. "So to anyone sitting at home, thinking it will never be them, that they will never make it... play harder, work harder... *love* harder, and the rest will follow."

My hand slid into my dress slacks pocket, my body vibrating with restless energy. I felt like I'd been standing up there for an hour, not ten minutes. But there was still one person left to thank.

Rubbing a hand over my jaw, I forced down the wave of emotion threatening to bring me to my knees. "Before I say goodnight, there's someone else I need to thank tonight." My eyes found her down in the audience. "Two years ago, I believed the only way to get to the top was with rigid determination and narrowed focus. I won't sugarcoat it; I was a bit of an arrogant ass. But then Felicity barreled into my life and showed me it didn't have to be like that. Love doesn't make us weak, it makes us strong. Football will always be the dream, always. But what's a dream without a pretty girl by your side and a future laid out before you?"

I left the stand and walked along the far aisle to Felicity. Her eyes widened, filled with fresh tears. "J- Jason, what the hell are you doing?" She pressed a hand to her mouth as I dropped to one knee and presented her with the ring box I'd been carrying all evening.

"Felicity Charlotte Giles, you once permanently inked my stamp on your skin, but what I didn't tell you that day was, you're permanently tattooed on me too. You own me, babe. And I wasn't kidding when I said we're endgame."

Mya and Hailee let out little shrieks of approval as I flipped the lid.

"So, what do you say, Giles? Want to really make this a night to remember and say yes to marrying me?" The words coiled through me, filling me with so much emotion I had to blink the tears right out of my eyes.

"You're crazy." She slid off her chair, kneeling with me.

"Crazy about you." I grinned. "I know this season has been hard. I know the next two seasons will probably be equally as hard. But I thought that maybe if you're wearing my number as well as my ring, it would help you remember that I'm all in, babe. I'm so fucking in."

"Yes," she cried. "Yes, I'll marry you."

I'd won a ring once. A championship ring in my senior year of high school. It had meant everything to me at the time; but this, right here, sliding the princess cut diamond band onto Felicity's finger showed me it was nothing compared to this moment.

Because no matter where my football career took me; no matter if I entered the draft and landed a spot with an NFL team, it would be nothing without this girl by my side.

Football was the dream.

But Felicity?

She was my endgame.

PART II

Junior Year

11

Asher

"I can't believe it's junior year already," Mya let out a small sigh as the six of us sat around the electric fire out on the terrace on the roof of our building. Summer was slowly retreating, giving way to the crisp mornings and cool evenings.

It had been a crazy year. Jason and Felicity had gotten engaged after he won the Heisman Trophy, seven months ago. Their relationship had only gotten stronger after he put that ridiculously big diamond on her finger. I couldn't speak for Cameron, but I felt the pressure. We were still young—we still had two years of college left—but I wanted that.

I wanted to bind Mya to me in all the ways that mattered.

She'd rip me a new one though if I even tried to get down on one knee. She wanted us to enjoy life, to make the most of college and classes and football. If anything, I was the Flick in our relationship; wondering when this smart, gorgeous, humble girl was going to slip through my fingers. But I wasn't about to confess that to her or my friends, so I pulled her closer and kissed her hair, reminding myself of how fucking lucky I was.

"You ready for another season?" I asked Jase.

"You know it."

It had been a summer of football camps, some time visiting my folks and Mya's aunt back in Rixon, and a week at the Hamptons.

"You think the Wolverines can go all the way this season?" I asked Cam.

He gave me a half-shrug. "Who knows?"

"What the fuck is that supposed to mean?"

"Ash," Hailee warned, and I frowned.

What the hell was happening right now?

"Xander got upset when we left," Cam blew out a long breath, running a hand down his face. "He said some things."

"Shit, man, I didn't realize." Xander was almost seven and he adored his older brother to the point where he struggled with Cam being away so much.

"It's just hard, ya know? I want to be there for him, but I'm not always going to be around."

"It's not your fault." Hailee rubbed his arm.

"Sorry for being a dick." I apologized.

"Nah, it's not you, it's me," he murmured.

Being an only child, I didn't get what it felt like to carry the responsibility of a sibling, especially a little kid who had already been through so much.

He still had nightmares about his mom being sick, even though everyone thought he was too young to remember. I'd only seen Xander a handful of times since we graduated, but the last time I'd seen the little guy, he'd seemed lost. Wearing a vacant look, he'd barely smiled unless his big brother was giving him his full attention.

I knew Cameron carried a lot of guilt over leaving. His heart torn between the girl he loved and the little brother he wanted to protect.

"But your mom is okay, right?"

"Yeah, she's fine. But she and my dad are both at a loss about what to do with him. He's so... different."

"He'll be okay," Hailee said. "As soon as we can, we'll bring him out to Michigan and show him the sights again."

Cameron leaned down and kissed her. "Thank you."

"Are you excited about classes, Mya?" Flick asked, changing the subject to safer shores.

"I can't freakin' wait. Although I wish it was senior year so I could jump into field practice."

"I'm not going to lie, I'm a little scared about clinical practice."

"Nah, babe." Jason hooked his arm around Felicity. "You've got this."

"And hey, at least *tutor boy* will be around to help you if things get too much." I smirked and Jase flipped me off.

"Really, you went there?" A low growl rumbled in his chest.

"Joke. I'm joking."

"Yeah, well it doesn't matter," Felicity said. "Darcy graduated. He's no longer at Penn."

"Thank fuck," Jason murmured, and she elbowed him in the ribs.

"Without Darcy I probably would have flunked my classes."

"You would have figured it out."

The two of them started bickering quietly while the rest of us watched the flames lick the inky sky. There was something about ending the summer with your girl and best friends and stepping into a new year. It was a tradition we'd started the summer before college. One I intended on keeping. We may have had less and less time for one another now we were all at college, but when we came together it was like no time had passed.

"What are you thinking?" Mya brushed the hair from my eyes.

"Just how perfect this is."

"Another year," she sighed.

"Another year closer to the rest of our lives together."

"Ash..."

"I know. No rush, right?" I touched my head to hers.

"We have time." Mya brushed her lips over mine and I was a goner.

There wasn't anything I wouldn't do for this girl. If she wanted time, I'd give it to her.

So long as she knew she was my forever.

———

"God, Asher, it's—"

"Fuck, babe, I know." I thrust up inside Mya again, curling my hand around her hip, encouraging her to ride me harder... Faster... *Deeper.*

"You feel incredible." Leaning up on my elbows, I took one of her perfect tits in my hand and flicked my tongue over the dusky bud. Mya cried out, throwing her head back as I sucked and laved, teasing her sensitive skin with my teeth.

I wanted to mark her, to brand her permanently as mine. I'd never been a possessive asshole, at least not like Jason... until Mya came along.

I couldn't explain my need to possess and consume her. I wanted her tied to me in every way possible.

Heart, mind, body, and soul.

I guess you could say I was a lot to handle. But Mya loved me. She loved our life together. And we openly talked about the future.

"Fuck." She ground her hips slower, rocking in tortuous circles, making my body tremble with pleasure. "Fuuuuck."

Mya smirked, aware of the power she held over me. I'd gladly handed over my balls to her when I'd chosen Temple —chosen *her*—over my place at Pittsburgh. But I wouldn't have changed it for the world.

When you'd grown up under the stifling expectations of my father, having something—*someone*—to call your own, to love and cherish and worship... well, it was a rare thing of beauty.

Need burned through me and I flipped Mya onto her back, slamming inside her, so deep she cried my name. Threading our fingers together, I pressed our hands beside her head as I pulled out and rocked back in, over and over, driving us to the point of sweet ecstasy.

"I'm close." She raked her fingers down my spine,

moaning into my ear as I trailed hot wet kisses down her throat.

A familiar tingling started at the bottom of my spine just as Mya pulled me deeper into her body, locking her legs around my hips and shuddering around me.

I kissed her deeply as I fucked her into complete submission.

Nothing... *nothing* would ever feel as good as this.

Except maybe our wedding night.

Or the day I watched her birth our kids into the world.

Okay, so I was a little more than ahead of the game. But I was a Bennet. I had a game plan. One that included me and Mya and a happily-ever-after.

Mya

Sunlight framed Asher's face, making him look angelic. Although the way he'd loved my body last night was nothing short of sinful. A shiver ran through me just thinking about how he'd flipped me onto my back and fucked me as if it was the last time he would ever get to be inside me.

I let my fingers linger on his chest, tracing his cut abs, loving how warm his skin was. Sometimes it was hard to believe this was my life. I was halfway through my bachelor's in social work and living in an amazing building with my boyfriend. It was a far cry from life in Fallowfield Heights. But I'd earned it. I'd made sacrifices and worked my ass off to get here.

Asher, and all that came with being his girlfriend, was just the icing on the cake.

"You should probably move a little lower." His voice was thick with sleep.

"No can do, I'm meeting Faith for a run." I dipped my head and kissed him. It was supposed to be a chaste gentle peck, but when I tried to pull away, Asher buried his hand in my thick curls and captured my lips with his.

"Good morning," he breathed, finally letting me up for air.

"Morning." I smiled. I couldn't help it. I was one of those annoying girls now, sickeningly in love with her boyfriend. A football player no less.

"Are you going to the gym with the guys?"

"Yeah, I think Aiden wants us there."

I kissed him again. "Well, don't work too hard."

"What do you want to do later? I was thinking we could get dinner at Dukes or we could stay home and Netflix and Chill." His brows waggled.

"Or... we could go to The Hideout for open mic night."

"Yeah?" He frowned. "You enjoyed that?"

"What?" I batted his chest. "Faith is on the roster tonight and I want to support her."

"But what about supporting me and my very, *very*," he grabbed my hand and cupped it over his morning wood, "real problem?"

"You're insufferable," I chuckled.

"No, I'm just a guy in love with a girl." Asher nuzzled my neck, sucking and licking.

"I know what you're doing." I tried to push him away.

"I have no idea what you mean." He sucked harder, making blood rush to the surface, bruising me.

"Ash, you'll make me look like—"

"You're mine. I'll make you look like you're mine."

With a heavy eye roll, I untangled myself from him and climbed out of bed before he could grab me again.

"Tell Faith we'll be there," he called, just as I disappeared into the bathroom.

Every time. I smiled to myself.

Every damn time.

———

"So you're coming tonight, right?" Faith pressed her hands to her knees, breathing deeply.

"Wouldn't miss it for the world." I smiled.

Faith and I had been friends since our first day of freshman year. We'd met in orientation and never looked back. Like me, she wanted to make a difference: to work with those less fortunate, and help kids flourish, despite their often dire circumstances.

Felicity and Hailee aside, she was my best friend. So of course, I was going to be at the poetry slam night at The Hideout later.

"Asher's coming too."

"You know, it's cute that he wants to support you supporting me, but it wouldn't hurt him to relax the reins now and again."

My brows furrowed. "What's that supposed to mean?"

"I'm just saying, he's like your shadow. It's... a lot."

We stretched our calves before breaking into a gentle jog through Fairmount Park.

"We enjoy each other's company. Is that such a crime?"

"No." She chuckled, but it did little to ease the knot in my stomach. "I just think it would be nice to hang out occasionally without Asher tagging along."

"We hang out, Faith." We hung out all the time with the rest of the people from our class.

"Forget I said anything." She brushed me off, but her words lingered.

Before the summer, Faith had ended her relationship with her childhood sweetheart Max. She said they'd outgrown each other. I knew she'd embarked on a summer of self-discovery and sex with strangers, but I hadn't expected her to come back so judgmental of my relationship with Asher.

Awkward silence followed us as we jogged under the leafy canopy of the oak and ash trees.

"I know things have been hard since you and Max—"

"Honestly?" She shrugged. "I feel like a new woman. I'd been with Max since junior year in high school and I hadn't realized how suffocating our relationship was until I walked away."

"I'm glad you're in a better place, Faith, I am. But some of us are happy in our relationships."

"Asher is a total babe, and he's rich. Trust me, I get it."

She got it?

My stomach sank. Is that what she thought? That I was with Asher for his money?

"I love Asher," I said defiantly, annoyed at myself for

even feeling the need to defend our relationship. "It has nothing to do with how wealthy his family is."

"I know you do." She shot me a weak smile. "But do you really think you'll go the distance?" Faith picked up her pace and left me trailing behind...

Wondering what the fuck had just happened.

12

Asher

"You don't have to come tonight, you know?" Mya said, making me frown.

"What? Why wouldn't I want to come?"

"I know poetry isn't your thing and I think some of the guys from our class are going to be there. You'll probably be bored."

I glanced over at her. "Are you trying to get rid of me?"

"What? No! I'm just giving you an out." She shrugged as if it was nothing.

An out?

What the actual fuck?

"We always spend Sunday together," I said.

"I know and I love it, I do." Mya came toward me and I opened my legs, letting her slip between them. Linking her hands behind my neck, she gazed down at me. "I just didn't want you to think you have to come."

"Is everything okay?" My brows furrowed deeper. "You're acting weird."

"Everything's fine." Her lips pursed a little and I knew everything was not fucking fine.

"You want me to come, right?"

Shit. I sounded like a pussy. But we always spent Sunday's together during the semester. It was our way of making time for each other when the weeks got busy and our schedules got hectic.

"Of course." Mya brushed her lips over mine, but I intensified the kiss, sliding my tongue into her mouth and tangling it with hers.

"Keep kissing me like that and we'll never make it out of here."

"Now there's an idea," I chuckled.

"I can't believe it's junior year already." She exhaled a small sigh.

"Believe it, baby." I kissed her again.

"Okay, I'm going to finish getting ready and then we can head out." Mya's hand lingered on my shoulder and then she walked away, disappearing into the bathroom.

My cell phone vibrated, and I plucked it off the coffee table, scanning the text message.

Diego: A few of us are hanging out later, you should come.

Me: It's Sunday. Got plans with Mya.

My teammates knew the deal.

. . .

Diego: You are so fucking pussy whipped...

Me: Never claimed to be anything else.

I smirked, running a hand over my jaw. The guys liked to bust my balls about Mya, about how serious I was about her. But I didn't give a fuck. I loved her. And I'd almost lost her once... there was zero chance of me ever losing her again. I didn't care that it was college, that it was supposed to be the time for partying and sowing your wild oats. Football wasn't my life like it was for so many of my friends, like it was for Jason. I loved playing and I enjoyed the brotherhood and camaraderie, but it wasn't the end goal for me. I had zero intention of going pro.

Diego: Well, you know where we'll be if you change your mind.

Wasn't going to happen but I appreciated him getting off my back about it.

———

The Hideout was crammed but Faith had reserved a table upfront for Mya and a couple of their other friends. It was an eclectic crowd. Preppy types with something to prove. The stoners, all high on weed, free love, and peace. The drama students all desperately trying to get their big break. Then Mya and her friends; the ones out to change the world and make a difference. There wasn't a jock in sight, but I didn't care because although football was a big part of my life, it didn't define me. I had ambitions and plans just as much as the rest of the people here.

"You know, Asher," Rex, one of Mya's friends said, "it's nice you support her passions."

I frowned at that. "Is that not what two people in a relationship usually do?" Taking a long pull on my beer, I offered him a tight smile.

"Of course." His laughter came out strangled. "I just meant, what with you being on the football team and all."

"We're not all the conceited, selfish, shallow guys you paint us to be, ya know?" My lips thinned.

"I didn't... that's not..." He pulled at the collar on his sweater. "That came out wrong."

"Relax, Rexy boy. I'm secure enough to not give a crap about your stellar opinion of me."

"Asher, I didn't..." He released a heavy sigh, running a hand down his face. "You really love her, huh?"

I looked at the guy, *really* looked at him. He'd only really migrated into Mya's group last year, but I'd been around Rex enough times to know the dude had confidence issues.

"Have I ever given you or the gang reason to think I don't?" My brow arched.

The 'gang' was tight. They looked out for each other,

hung out a lot, and shared the highs and lows of their emotionally demanding course. And until today, I'd never really questioned my position among them. But in less than a couple of hours, Mya had suggested that I didn't have to tag along, and now Rex was acting like I didn't belong.

Not how I saw the beginning of semester going.

As if she heard my thoughts, Mya glanced over at me and mouthed, "You good?"

I nodded, because I wasn't about to let Rex, or anyone else for that matter, know how I really felt.

Maybe I should have taken Diego up on his offer after all.

Faith took the stage and we all clapped. Aside from Hailee and Felicity, she was Mya's best friend. Freshman and sophomore year, we had hung out with her and her ex-boyfriend a lot. It had been nice, having another couple on campus to do things with. But Faith and Max had broken up before the end of sophomore year and that was that.

"Hey everyone. I'm Faith and this poem is called Freedom..."

Freedom is the power to breathe. To live and grow and feel.

Freedom is the power to speak. To think and consider and be.

Freedom is the power to love. To ask and give and hold.

You told me you loved me, but you hurt me the most. You took all that freedom and stripped it from my soul, leaving me weak and ruined.

You gave me your word, you promised me the world... and then stole it away in the blink of an eye.

Freedom is the power to change. To realize I'd become who you wanted me to be. Not who I needed to be.

Freedom is the right to say no. To protect my heart and body and soul and refuse to submit.

Freedom is the me saying I'm done... you don't get to hold all the cards anymore.

I'm free.

And you're no one.

———————————————

The room was silent, the pain and passion in Faith's words rippling in the air, making it thick and heavy. She was Mya's friend, not mine, but it didn't take much to figure out she was talking about her ex. I shifted uncomfortably in my chair. I knew Max. I'd witnessed them as a couple: saw the way he'd loved her, the way he'd made her laugh. He'd wanted more and she hadn't. That's what Faith had told Mya, so the fact she was standing up there, publicly dissecting their relationship, and making him sound like a possessive asshole, left a sour taste in my mouth.

From the earsplitting applause she received, it was apparent no one else agreed with my assessment of her poem.

"Holy. Shit. Girl," Mya said, "that was awesome."

"I've been feeling inspired." Her twinkling gaze landed on mine and she narrowed her eyes. But as quickly as it was there, it was gone, as she lapped up the praise from her friends.

"Rex, help me get the drinks in?" Faith crooked her finger at him, and he went willingly.

Mya slid into his seat and looped her arms around my neck. "What did you think?"

"It was... a little harsh."

She reared back, confusion clouding her eyes. "What do you mean?"

"Come on, babe. She made Max out to be a complete asshole."

"It wasn't necessarily about Max."

"It was so about him. She dumped him, and yet she stood up there making it sound like he was some possessive narcissist, which we both know couldn't be further from the truth."

"Huh. I guess I didn't think about it like that."

"He wanted more, and Faith freaked."

"It's just slam poetry, Ash. You don't need to get so upset over it."

"I'm not upset," I sighed, running a hand over my head. "I just think it's a little unfair."

"You know what she's like." Mya brushed her nose over mine, stealing a kiss. "She's all for girl power and independence."

"And making her ex out to sound like a total asshole apparently," I grumbled.

"It's their business. Who are we to say how someone should or shouldn't feel? Max was a good guy, but he was kind of intense, always glued to her side. I guess she felt smothered."

"Is that what earlier was about?" I asked, the chips falling into place with a resounding *thud*.

"What?" Mya's gaze widened.

"When you said I didn't have to come tonight. Did Faith say something to you about me?"

"I..." Mya let out a small breath. "Not exactly," she

admitted. "She's just in a weird place and wants to make the most of her newfound freedom."

"So she did say something to you?"

Un-fucking-believable.

"She didn't mean anything by it."

"Did you?" My body vibrated with a sense of impending doom. I couldn't really explain it, but I knew this wasn't going to end well. Yet, for some reason, I couldn't let it go.

"Asher, stop... this is silly."

"I don't think it is," I said.

First Mya, then Diego and Rex, and now Faith's stupid poem.

"Do you feel smothered by me?" Before I could stop them, the words spilled from my lips, and Mya's breath hitched.

"Where is all this coming from?"

"Answer the question, Mya," I ground out. The chatter and laughter went on around us, but it barely penetrated the roar of blood between my ears.

"You're being ridiculous." Her gaze went over my shoulder. "They're coming back. Please don't make this into something it isn't."

But the seed was planted, and I couldn't shake the feeling, I wasn't really welcome here tonight after all.

Standing, I shoved my hands in my pockets. "I'm going to hang out with Diego and the guys. I'll see you back at the apartment later."

"Leaving so soon?" Faith shot me a smug look.

"Yeah," I replied. "I guess it wasn't my scene after all."

And then I got the hell out of there.

Mya

"I should go after him." My chest constricted as I watched Asher walk away from us. He'd been so upset, so weird over Faith's poem.

But then, I'd screwed up earlier.

I'd seen the dejection in his eyes when I'd suggested he didn't have to come.

God, I should never have said anything. We always spent Sunday together. And I loved it. But Faith was in a weird place and Asher was a lot like Max. When he loved, he loved with his entire being. It had taken some getting used to, being the center of his universe, but I never felt smothered.

Overwhelmed sometimes, sure, but never smothered.

"Let him go." Faith shrugged, taking a long slurp of her drink. "You guys can kiss and make up later."

"She's right, you know," Bella, our other friend, said. "A little time and space never hurt... besides, makeup sex." She waggled her brows.

"Ugh, no thanks." Faith rolled her eyes. "Max was always so clingy after an argument."

"So, the poem," I asked, changing the subject. "Was that—"

"About Max? Yeah... he was just so stifling sometimes. It was like I couldn't breathe. He'd want to talk about our life after college, having a family and settling down..."

"He thought you were the one," Rex said, frowning.

"I guess. But it's college... we're supposed to find ourselves and spread our wings. Not... clip them."

"It's why I stick to my three-date rule." Bella nodded.

"But what if you met the right person?" I asked.

"Like you and Asher?" She gave me a warm smile. Unlike Faith who glowered.

"What?" I glared back.

"Asher is a nice guy, but do you really think he's the one?"

"Faith," Rex hissed under his breath.

"No, it's okay," I said, feeling a trickle of irritation up my spine. "Let her make her point."

"All I'm saying is, you met in high school, under... difficult circumstances. You went through something huge together. That kind of trauma can bind two people together. We see it all the time in class. That shared experience can become a dependency... a crutch. But unless you give yourself time and space to come to terms with that trauma, you can't really know who you are or what you want."

Faith had a point. We'd studied enough about attachment, shared trauma, and trauma bonding for me to know that people often did mistake shared trauma for compatibility. But what me and Asher had wasn't some product of our experiences.

When my ex, Jermaine, had found me in Rixon and shot Asher's mom, part of me had felt sure Asher would never be able to forgive me. At the time, I hadn't been sure *I* would ever forgive myself. But Asher loved me *in spite of* that. He'd done nothing but prove to me he was in.

All in.

When I didn't answer, Faith let out an exasperated breath. "Look, all I'm saying is, we're halfway into college. Do you really want to spend your entire college experience tied to another person who may or may not end up being the one? Because I sure as hell don't."

I pressed my lips together, considering her words. Asher had gone against his father's plans for him and followed me to Temple University.

He put me first every single time.

Above the team. Above his family and friends.

Faith was wrong. I didn't need to spend the next two years questioning anything. Because I knew. In my heart of hearts, I knew how Asher felt about me. And I knew how I felt about him.

"You're wrong," I said, standing.

"Seriously? You're going after him?" Faith gawked at me, while Bella gave me a discreet thumbs up.

"I get Max wasn't it for you, but Asher is it for me. You're one of my best friends and I'll always be here for you... but don't project your shit onto me, okay?"

Faith smothered a gasp and I offered her a weak smile. "I'll see you in class."

I didn't wait around to hear her reply. I had to go after my guy.

13

Asher

"Yo, man. We weren't expecting you." Diego swaggered over to me. He had an Owls ball cap pulled on backwards and his jeans slung low on his hips.

"Do you ever wear a shirt?" I asked, meeting his fist bump with my own.

"And deny the ladies all this?" He swept a hand down his cut abs. "Nah, bro. So, what's up? I thought you and Mya had plans?"

"We did." I pressed my lips together, smothering a groan.

"Oh shit, trouble in paradise?"

"Honestly, I don't know what the fuck happened. One minute, everything was fine, the next..."

"You need a drink. Yo, Broderick," he hollered over his shoulder. "Get my guy, Asher, a beer."

Ten seconds later, Broderick appeared. "Hey, man."

"What's up?" I gave him a small nod.

"Not a lot. Just shooting some pool and deciding who to take for a ride tonight." He smirked, and the two of them high-fived, laughing and jostling each other.

"Ash and Mya had a fight," Diego said.

139

"Oh shit. You need me to hook you up? Jada is here and she brought plenty of friends."

"I'm good, thanks." Jada was a cheerleader and more than happy to service the football team.

"You need to relax, man," he said. "Have a drink. Get your dick suck—"

"Do not finish that sentence," a familiar voice said, and Diego let out a low whistle.

"Mya?" I turned to meet her narrowed gaze. "What are you—"

"Can we talk?" Her brow went up.

"We'll give the two of you some space." Diego dragged Broderick away.

"You left," she said.

"I didn't think I was welcome there." I rubbed my bottom lip, hating the distance between us.

If Cameron and Jason were here, I knew they would tell me to grow some balls. But I'd always worn my heart on my sleeve, I wasn't about to change now.

"Ash." She inched closer, so close I could smell her perfume. "What has gotten into you?"

I reached for her, but Mya batted my hand away, pressing her palms flat against my chest and pushing me into the wall.

"You knew what you were signing on for with me," I said. "I'm intense and needy and so fucking gone for you."

"Faith said some things..." Her eyes glittered with emotion. "But she doesn't get it. No one does. The way I feel about you. The way you make me feel..." Mya leaned in, letting her mouth hover over mine. "You're it for me, Asher Bennet."

"Yeah?" My throat felt dry, my heart beating hard beneath my ribcage.

She nodded. "I'm sorry I made you doubt how I feel about us."

My hand slipped around Mya's neck, holding her there and touching my head to hers. "I'm sorry I overreacted about Faith's poem. But the idea you might not feel the same—"

"I do." A grin spread across her gorgeous face. "And I'm right here."

I captured her lips, pushing my tongue into her mouth. She tasted so fucking good. I wanted to take my time exploring every inch of her.

"Erm, babe, unless you want an audience, maybe we should take this back to our place." Mya buried her face into the crook of my neck, and I wound my hands around her body.

"I love you."

"I love you too, Asher." She lifted her eyes to mine. "So much."

"This year is going to be amazing. I promise."

"I know." I saw nothing but complete conviction there, and it was such a fucking relief.

"And I promise to give you space, even if I do hate every second that I'm away from you." My lips curved but I meant every single word.

"Well, I promise to always come back to you. How does that sound?"

Ducking my head, I brushed my nose over hers. "It sounds pretty damn perfect."

Mya

"Jesus, babe," Asher rasped as I ran my tongue along his shaft. He'd already made love to me once and again in the shower. But there was something about tonight's events that made me crave him.

His hands slid into my curls, guiding my mouth deeper over him. "That feels so fucking good."

Despite his vice-like hold on me, Asher let me set the pace. After more than two-and-a- half years together, I knew exactly how to bring him to the edge. My hand jacked him slowly in rhythm with my tongue, as I licked and flicked, sucking him like a popsicle.

"Fuck, Mya..." he choked out as I took his dick deeper, relishing the clean taste of him.

Our eyes connected, and I held his stare as I ran my lips up and down, swirling my tongue over the tip. "I'm close..." His grip on my hair relaxed a little and I knew I had him right where I wanted him.

Asher's head rolled back, a string of cuss words leaving his lips on breathy moans. I sucked him harder... *deeper*... flattening my tongue against his shaft and bobbing my head up and down.

"Fuuuuck," Asher went to pull away, but I tightened my hold on him, not letting him go until I'd swallowed down every last drop.

Licking my lips, I sat up.

"Do you have any idea how fucking sexy you look like that?" He wound his hand around my wrist and tugged me forward. I went willingly, letting Asher pull me across his body. He leaned down, kissing me hard, not caring that he could taste himself on my tongue. Desire pulsed through me, but it was late, and we had class in the morning.

Asher must have had the same thought because instead of deepening the kiss, he rolled me over and spooned me from behind, wrapping his big body around mine. "We should fight more often," he teased.

"That wasn't a fight, babe. A fight requires raised voices, some smashed glasses, and a fist or two."

He chuckled. "My little fighter."

"What we had earlier was... a moment."

"A moment. I can live with that. Let's just not make a habit of it." He snuggled me tighter.

Sometimes, when we were like this, it was hard to believe this was my life. The girl from Fallowfield Heights living in a prestigious apartment building in the city with her rich football-playing boyfriend.

Asher was everything I never wanted... and everything I never knew I needed.

"Penny for your thoughts?" He ran his nose along my shoulder.

"Just thinking how I ended up here."

"You need me to remind you? Because I can. I can spend the entire night reminding you of exactly why we're perfect for each other."

A shiver rolled through me at the intention in his words.

"Do you think it will always be like this?"

"I think life will have its ups and downs," he said, "but we'll get through whatever storms blow our way."

Glancing back, I smiled. "You always sound so sure of everything."

"Because I am. I love you, Mya. I love our life together. And I'm excited about what the future brings."

"Even if I want to stay in the city?" I wanted to work in the kinds of neighborhoods where I'd grown up. I wanted to make a difference to kids like me. I was one of the lucky ones, I got out. But so many kids thought their destinies were already decided for them. I wanted to show them there was always another way.

"I already told you, if that's what you want, that's what we'll do."

Rolling over, I stared up at Asher. He was so handsome, his features older and wiser, a young man on the cusp of great things. Turned out, Asher was whip smart like his father. He'd never wanted his father's life, but since starting his business degree two years ago, Asher had come to love the very thing he'd once resented.

"But what about your dad's business?"

"We'll figure it out. He's been wanting to expand. This could be the perfect opportunity. We have time." He kissed the end of my nose.

But two years was nothing. Once we threw ourselves into classes and the football season, junior year would pass us by in the blink of an eye, and we'd be one step closer to making the big decisions.

"Hey, Mya," Bella beckoned me over. "How are you... after, you know..."

"I'm good, thanks."

She nodded. "Have you seen Faith yet?"

"No, but honestly, it's not a big deal. She's entitled to her opinions, so long as she doesn't keep trying to—"

Bella widened her eyes and I turned just in time to greet Faith. "Hey," she said around a sheepish smile. "Can we talk for a second?"

"I'll just..." Bella left us to it.

"I'm sorry about last night. I had no right to—"

"No, you didn't," I said flatly. "Mine and Asher's relationship is just that, Faith, ours. I won't justify my decisions to you, and I don't expect you to judge me for my actions, the way I won't judge you for yours."

"You're right, you're totally right." She ran a hand through her silky red hair. "I'm just trying to be more in control of my life and sometimes it spills out. It won't happen again, I promise."

"Good."

"Did you find Asher?"

"Yeah."

"He probably hates me now, huh?"

"He doesn't hate you, Faith. He just doesn't understand you sometimes. Max was a good guy. I know you two had your differences, but I think the poem threw Ash for a loop."

"I can see that. To be honest, I think the poem was less

about Max and more about me and the pressure and expectations I put on myself."

"You'll get there, Faith. Don't be so hard on yourself."

I wanted to graduate and become a social worker, but not the same way Faith wanted it. She lived and breathed it, out to prove to everyone that she could make it. Her tenacity was inspiring, but I also wondered if it was impacting on her personal life. Asher hadn't been wrong, Max was a great guy. Solid and dependable with plans for the future. Most girls dreamed of meeting a guy like that. But not Faith, she'd run the second things got too serious.

"You're a good friend, Mya." She took my hand in hers. "Asher's lucky to have you." There was something in her eyes that looked a lot like regret, but I didn't ask.

Faith needed to work things out for herself.

"Come on," I said. "We should get to class."

Asher

"You made a quick exit last night," Diego said as we worked out next to each other.

"Yeah, we had shit to take care of."

"I bet you did." He shot me a knowing grin and I managed to flip him off.

"You know you're punching above your weight with Mya, right?"

"Fuck you, D." I chuckled. Of course I knew Mya was too good for me. But she was mine, and I didn't plan on giving her up for anything.

"I'm just busting your balls, she's a good girl. One of the best. She volunteering again at the center this semester?"

"Yeah, her field practice isn't until senior year, so she'll want to get all the hands-on experience she can."

"She's a better person than me. Some of those little punks would be cruising for a bruising with the way they talk to the staff there."

"It's what she wants to do," I said as if was that simple. And in a way, it was. But Diego was right, the New Hope Community Center worked with some of the most challenging kids living in and around Strawberry Mansion.

"Don't you ever worry about her being there?"

"What kind of question is that, D? Of course I fucking worry. She's my..." *Everything.*

Mya was my everything.

But she wanted to make a difference. She wanted to try to break the cycle of crime, drugs, and poverty so many of the kids in Philly found themselves in. It was important to her.

"It's not the nineteen-fifties," I said. "Women don't want to stay at home, raise the kids, and play Suzy Homemaker."

"Hey, my momma did just that and she's one of the best women I know." His eyes lit up with fondness.

Diego's mom was a great woman. I'd met her last year, when she'd showed up with Pastel de Elote for the team.

"Mya wants to make a difference," I said unsure who I was trying to convince more, myself or Diego.

"I hear ya, man. All I'm saying is, it's a crazy world out

there. Don't think I'd ever rest knowing my girl was in the thick of it."

My brows furrowed. He made it sound like Mya was going off to war.

But in some ways, she was.

The world needed people like Mya. People willing to put themselves on the line and advocate for those without a voice.

I was proud of her—so fucking proud.

But part of me would always worry. Because that's what you did when you loved someone.

14

Asher

"Looking good, Bennet," Coach yelled across the field as I ran drills with Diego and a hulk of a guy called Brian. "Run it again."

Our offensive line got into position, moving toward us like a well-oiled machine. I broke formation, tracking the wide receiver and making the lunge. Our bodies collided with a *thud* and we went down.

"Fuck, Bennet, you knocked the wind right out of my sails," Farrow said.

"Hell yeah, I did." I clambered up and offered him a hand up.

"Okay, hit the showers," Coach said, "you're done for the day."

I pulled off my helmet, dragging in a lungful of fresh air.

"You're looking good out there, bro," Diego said approaching me. We fist bumped but his eyes flickered over my shoulder. "You have company."

I turned to find Mya sitting in the bleachers. A smile tugged at the corner of my mouth. "I'll catch you in a bit."

He rolled his eyes, but I was already gone, heading in her direction.

"Hey," she said, coming down onto the field.

"This is a surprise." I kissed her cheek.

"I had a free period. I wanted to come and see you in action."

"Oh yeah? I thought football players didn't do it for you?" My voice was teasing.

"Oh, I don't know." Mya came closer, trailing a finger up my dirty jersey. "One football player caught my attention."

"Yeah?"

"Yeah, number six. He's looking—"

I grabbed her and started tickling her sides. "You want a piece of Farrow? I'll see if I can hook you up."

Her laughter wrapped around me like a warm blanket. "Okay, okay, you got me."

I eased up and leaned in to brush my nose over hers. "What are you really doing here?"

A knowing smile lifted the corner of her mouth. "Sally called. They need an extra hand tonight. They've got some new kids and want all hands on deck. I said I'd be there."

"Okay. Just be careful, okay?"

"Always." Mya kissed me.

"What time will you get done?"

My body stirred to life at her proximity. I was going to have a serious case of blue balls if she was going to be home late.

"I don't know. I wouldn't think any later than nine."

"Enough time for you to come home and show me just

how much you like football players then?" I smirked as my hands dipped around to her ass.

"Behave."

"With you? Never. I should probably go before Coach chews me out. But text me later?"

She nodded, taking a step backward. "Love you."

"I love you more." *So fucking much.*

I headed for the gym unable to hide the shit-eating grin lifting the corners of my mouth.

Yesterday had been rocky there for a moment, but everything had righted itself in the end. We'd had some of the best sex of my life. A new season was looming, and the team was looking stronger than ever. And I had a full schedule of classes I couldn't wait to get stuck into.

Life was great.

But there was still a small part of me that thought Mya underestimated just how much I loved her. I knew she wanted to stay in the city after graduation, and I knew she assumed I'd want to return to Rixon and help my old man with the company.

But she was wrong.

I just had to figure out a way to show her just how serious I was about our future together.

Mya

"Hey, sorry I'm late." I ran a hand through my hair and gave Sally, the New Hope Community Center coordinator, a big smile. "Tell me where you want me, and I'll jump straight in."

"We had some new kids signposted to the program, three brothers. They recently got placed into foster care. "The elder two, Jay and Mario are a little uncertain, but I've paired them up with Pat and Hershel."

"And the youngest?"

"Hugo, he's only six. His file says he's been a selective mute for the last two years."

My heart clenched. I'd seen a lot during my time volunteering with New Hope. It ran a *Big Brothers, Big Sisters* style program for kids in the foster care system, but instead of one-to-one activities, it operated at a community level. They held weekly sessions, and monthly group events, as well as providing ongoing support to the foster families and their charges.

"Here." Sally thrust a file at me. "It makes for difficult reading. Hugo is ready and waiting when you are."

I sat down on the leather bench in her office and flicked open the file.

Hugo Garcia aged six. Two siblings, Jay, aged eleven, and Mario, aged fourteen. Father unknown, mother known to authorities since Mario was just three, after she started turning tricks to make ends meet. A history of narcotic use, neglect, and poor school attendance.

"Jesus," I breathed, trying to get a hold on my emotions. No matter how many case files I read, it never got any easier.

"Jay and Mario have friends, they were able to get out of the house, but Hugo..." Sally's voice trailed off.

"It says here he likes football."

She nodded. "Came in clutching a stuffed Eagles mascot."

"I can work with that." At least, I hoped I could.

"If anyone can reach him, Mya, it's you."

Her words touched something inside me. All I wanted was to make a positive difference on the lives of the kids I encountered, so to have my mentor say that was everything.

I left Sally and went to find Hugo, spotting him the second I stepped into the main hall. A small kid with a head full of brown, curly hair, he watched the other kids and volunteers play a game of hacky sack.

I grabbed a soft football out of the box and made my way over to him. "Mind if I sit here?"

His silence and lack of eye contact spoke volumes. Instead, Hugo gave me a half-shrug and shifted along the bench.

"I'm Mya. I was hoping we could hang out."

More silence. But I didn't let it faze me. You had to have thick skin to work with these kids. Kids who had seen and experienced things no kid ever should.

"Is that Swoop?" I motioned to the tatty stuffed eagle in Hugo's hands. He was clutching onto the thing so tight I was surprised it hadn't ripped clean in two.

But he didn't respond.

"I'm not a huge fan, but my boyfriend plays for a college team. He's pretty good."

Hugo glanced at me, his stare so dull and lifeless it twisted my insides.

What had this poor kid seen to make him choose not to

communicate? To build walls so high he didn't know how to break through them? To choose isolation and solace over comfort and security?

"His name is Asher, he plays defense."

Hugo averted his gaze again, and the seed of hope that had flourished in my chest withered and died. But I'd keep pushing. Slowly and surely, I'd prove to this six-year-old with pain in his eyes that he could trust me.

———

Two weeks and three more sessions later, Hugo still refused to talk. He barely engaged in sessions, choosing to color or read a book in silence. His brothers had flourished, although Jay preferred the physical activities laid on by the center while Mario preferred the more creative ones.

"There you are." Asher looped his arms around me and pulled me against his chest as I added milk to my cereal.

"Sorry. I couldn't sleep."

He made me drop the spoon and turned me in his arms. "The kid?" His brows furrowed.

"He's just so... sad. It breaks my heart."

"Babe, we talked about this. You can't fix every kid who comes through the doors."

"I know." I bristled. "But you haven't seen him, Ash. He just sits there, completely closed off. I've spent almost ten hours with him, and he hasn't said a single word to me."

It was no time in the grand scheme of things, but it was the first time I'd worked with a selective mute before. It was hard not to let my own frustrations bleed over.

"You promised you wouldn't get too involved."

"I'm not," I snapped a little too harshly, and Asher arched a brow. "Sorry, I just—"

"You care, I get it. But some of these kids have experienced enough trauma to warrant a lifetime of therapy. You said he was getting professional support?"

I nodded. "Someone has been working with him at school. But so far, nothing."

"Know what I think?" He leaned down, touching his head to mine.

"What?"

"The little guy will talk when he's good and ready."

"I wish it were that simple." My shoulders sagged.

"Maybe he just needs a reason to talk."

"What do you mean?" It was my turn to frown.

"Maybe he needs some motivation, and I'm not talking getting a sticker or lollipop at the end of a session with the school shrink."

"Like a bribe?"

"Let's call it gentle persuasion."

"Actually," I said, an idea forming. "You might be onto something."

"Yeah?" Asher grinned. "And here was me thinking I was talking complete crap."

"There's this intervention a lot of schools use called the 'mystery motivator'. I might be able to adapt it."

"Sounds good. You said he likes football, right? Maybe we could arrange something once the season starts? Bring the kids out to a training session or even a game."

"You'd do that for them?"

"For you, babe. I'd do it for *you*." He kissed the end of my nose.

Ideas started firing off in my head. The only time Hugo even looked remotely interested in me was when I'd mentioned my boyfriend played college football. I'd tried to incorporate football into our activities and conversations as much as I could without coming on too strong. It was important to go at Hugo's pace, to gradually earn his trust.

"I'll talk to Sally and see what she thinks. Thank you." I threw my arms around his neck and kissed him. Asher grew hard against my stomach, and I eased back to look at him. "Seriously?" I smirked.

"What? My dick just so happens to be very, *very* attracted to you."

"Well, I hate to be a buzz kill..." I let my mouth linger on his, running my tongue over the seam of his lips. "But I have an early class." Slipping out from between Asher and the counter, I grabbed my bowl and sashayed away.

"You're killing me, Hernandez," he called after me.

"Love you too," I replied around a smile.

Because I did.

I loved Asher the way the stars loved the night.

Unconditionally.

Irrevocably.

Endlessly.

15

Asher

"Bennet, get in here, son," Coach Johnson called as I passed his office.

"What's up, Coach?"

"Just checking in. Wanted to see how you're feeling about the upcoming season?"

"I feel good, sir. The team is looking strong. I think we might have a real shot going into the playoffs."

"I agree. That kind of attention will bring scouts. You're a junior now, son. It's time to make some decisions about your future."

"Already made them, sir."

"I thought you might say that." He rubbed his jaw. "But I'd hoped to convince you to reconsider. When scouts come knocking, I'd really like your name on their list."

"I don't know what to tell you, sir. Going pro isn't in my plans."

"Well, shucks, Bennet. Never thought I'd see the day a talented young man such as yourself would give up a shot at the big leagues for a woman."

"She's not just any woman, sir." A smirk played on my lips.

me too, son. Me too. Now get out of here.

"No, son, I guess she's not." There was no malice in his expression; just mild disappointment, and a shit ton of respect.

"I'm sorry it wasn't the answer you'd hoped for, Coach."

"Me too, son. Me too. Now get out of here."

I gave him a nod and walked out of there. I knew the guys wouldn't understand, but it wasn't their life.

Back in senior year, at high school, I'd watched my mom almost die from a bullet meant for me. I'd watched the fear in my old man's eyes as he held the one woman who had always stood by his side, despite his flaws—and he had many. I'd made a promise to myself that day if Mya ever gave me a second chance—which she had—I would never do anything to jeopardize that.

Mya wanted a career, she wanted to make a difference. Her plans didn't include being with an NFL football player. And I didn't want anything that didn't include her. I wanted roots, a life together. I didn't want to be thrust into a world of football and fame.

Exiting the gym, I pulled out my cell and scrolled to my dad's number.

"Asher, this is a surprise," he said.

"Hey, Dad. I was hoping we could talk."

"Is everything okay, Son? You sound—"

"Everything's great. There's just some stuff I need your help with."

"Okay." He took a breath. "You want to talk about it now or should I drive up there?"

"Yeah?" I smiled.

There had been a time when Andrew Bennet was too focused on work to drop everything and come running. But he wasn't that guy anymore. I hadn't forgotten the way he'd treated Mya in the early stages of our relationship, or the cold-hearted bastard he'd been growing up, but I had found it within myself to forgive him. He loved Mya. She'd opened his eyes to so much more than a life of hard work and sparkling reputation. Between her and Mom, he was no longer the monster I had grown up with. I'd earned a second chance with Mya, so it seemed only fair, I gave him one.

"Of course, Asher. How about I come this evening? We can go to that quaint little place you took me and your mother last time we visited."

"The Hideout? Actually, I have somewhere else in mind."

"Whatever you want. Will Mya be joining us?"

"She has a shift at the center, but she might be able to join us after, if you're still around."

"I can always make time for Mya." I smiled at that. "I'll see you both later."

We hung up and I checked my wristwatch.

Only five hours until I could start putting Operation Future into action.

Mya

"It's good to see you again, Hugo," I said, sitting down beside him. He was busy coloring in another picture of Swoop, the Eagles mascot. Sally had printed a bunch off for him. It was his favorite activity; one of the only activities he engaged with.

"That looks great," I added when he didn't acknowledge me. "I thought we could try something different today. I'm hoping you'll like it." I placed the blank cards and envelopes down in front of me. I'd spoken to Sally about my idea and she and Hugo's social worker were all for it.

He finally lifted his dull brown eyes to mine. "Hi, there," I said, giving him a soft smile. "Would you like me to tell you about the activity I thought we could do?"

He gave me an imperceptible shrug, but I took it as permission.

Hope unfurled in my stomach. I didn't want to get overexcited, but this was huge. I gently pushed a card and pen toward him. "So, I know how you love football. Your brothers have been telling me all about it." I winked and his little brows furrowed. "They said you want to be like Fletcher Cox when you're older?"

He stared back at me with a blank expression, but I kept going. "I want you to think about football for a minute. I want you to think about the way it makes you feel and why you love it so much, and then, when you're ready, I want you to write one wish down on the card. It can be anything to do with football, okay?"

Seconds ticked by as Hugo stared at the blank card. I didn't push. I didn't speak. I just sat there quietly, waiting. For this to work, he had to engage with the process... he had to own it.

After a few minutes, I was worried he wasn't going to

bite. But then, slowly, Hugo picked up the pen and began drawing. His grip was shaky, the lines messy and unintelligible. But we could figure out the details later. I just needed an idea to work with.

"Finished?" I asked once he'd stopped drawing. He gave me his sad eyes again and nodded. It was a small action, but it was something.

"You did great, Hugo. Do you mind if I take a look?"

He slid the card across to me. Thankfully, I could just make out the football field and huge bird-like man in the center.

My lips curved as I realized what he was telling me. "You'd like to go to the Lincoln Financial Field and meet Swoop, huh?"

Emotion welled inside me. It was something so innocent and pure, it made my heart ache.

"Well, I can't promise anything," because that was the number one rule of working with kids—no promises—"but I'm going to see what I can do, okay?"

A flicker of interest passed over his face.

"But you have to do something for me too."

His expression fell.

"I'm going to put your wish in this envelope and we're going to keep it over there on that bookcase." I pointed at shelves across the room. "See." Taking the pen, I stuffed the card inside the envelope and wrote 'Hugo' across the front. "It's going to stay right there... and when you're ready to try to make it come true, all you have to do is ask me."

His eyes widened a little, fear glittering there.

"I know it's scary," I spoke gently. "I know you haven't

spoken to anyone in a really long time, but you don't have to be afraid anymore, okay? The Hansons are a good family. They want you and your brothers to feel safe.

"It doesn't have to be today or the next time we meet, but I'd really like it, if, one day, you use your voice to ask me for the envelope."

Hugo studied me, his murky brown eyes fixed on mine. I wanted to know what he was thinking, what he saw when he looked at me. But I knew it wasn't that simple. In this field, patience was your best friend. Progress was often made in baby steps, and just when you thought you were moving forward, something would happen to set you back again.

"Do you think you can give it a try? I'll put the envelope over there for safe keeping, and when you're ready to ask me for it, I'll be right here waiting."

Hugo shifted on his chair and I hated that it was because I was pushing him into a state of discomfort. But I'd read up a lot on selective mutism and it often came hand in hand with social anxiety disorder. Overcoming it wasn't going to be easy, but he was still young. With the right interventions and support, there was no reason why Hugo couldn't slowly regain his speech and confidence.

But then he looked at me again, and although he didn't nod, I saw his answer.

Hugo would try.

And I would wait.

Asher

"I'm sorry I missed your dad," Mya said as we lay in bed.

"It's okay. Rough night?" She'd gotten home a little after ten.

"I offered to stay and help Sally clean up."

"Of course you did." I smiled, stroking her warm skin. "How did it go with the kid?"

"I'm not sure yet. But I'm hoping it'll reach him." She snuggled closer. "So what brought your dad to Philly?"

"I wanted to talk to him, and he offered to drive up."

Mya rolled onto her stomach, gazing up at me. "What did you need to talk to him about?" Her nose scrunched up.

"Things."

"Things." Her brow arched with suspicion, and I chuckled.

"I wanted to feel him out about opening a second branch of his business here."

Her eyes went wide. "You did?"

"I was serious about what I said, Mya. You want to put down roots here, and if I'm going to work for the family business, that doesn't just happen overnight. We'd need to find premises, employ a team, source clients."

"Wow, you've really given this a lot of thought."

I reached for one of her spiral curls and twirled it around my finger. "Coach asked me today about going pro. Said I have a shot—"

"Ash," she frowned, "I don't want you to give up that dream for me."

"It isn't just about you. It's about me too. And honestly,

I don't want it. I love football, but it's not my life. You are."
Her breath caught, but I wasn't done. "I know we're young,
and I know you probably think I'm crazy for even talking
about starting a family, but I want that. I want a life with
you."

"Actually..." Mya pressed her lips together and looked
up at me through her thick lashes. "I've been doing some
thinking myself..." She hesitated. "How do you feel about
fostering?"

"As in fostering kids?"

"No, puppies." She rolled her eyes. "Of course, kids. I
was talking to Sally tonight and she was telling me all about
the family who have taken in Hugo and his brothers, and
what they're doing... it's incredible. I always thought the
way I could help and make a difference was to be out there
in the community, working at grass roots level. But maybe
this is something else to consider."

"I'm not going to lie, babe, I don't know the first thing
about fostering. Don't you have to be settled? Have a good
job, a house, that kind of thing?"

"There is eligibility criteria, yes. But it isn't as rigid as
you think. You have to be over twenty-one and have a stable
living arrangement, but the rest is pretty flexible."

"Fostering, huh?" I didn't know how to feel about
opening up my home to a kid who wasn't mine. I'd always
imagined we'd start a family with a baby, *our* baby.

"It's not something we have to decide or even talk about
yet. I just think it's something I might want to do one day."

"You have a big heart, Mya Hernandez." I brushed my

thumb over her cheek, letting it linger on the pillow of her lip.

"I just want to help. You came into my life when I needed someone. I'd like to think I can pay that forward one day."

Well, shit. When she put it like that... but fostering? That was huge, and we were so young.

"I don't want this to be another issue between us," she said as if she could hear my thoughts. "I was just saying it's something I'd like to think about, one day."

"I know."

But I also knew Mya, and once she got something in her mind... Yeah, this wasn't going away anytime soon.

I could give Mya a lot of things: money, love, a happy life... but could I give her this?

There was only one thing for it. I needed a beer and some guy time with my best friend.

16

Asher

"Hey, thanks for coming." I got up to greet Jason. We guy-hugged before taking a seat at the bar.

"Anytime. What's up?"

"I... fuck, I don't even know where to start."

"Is everything okay? With Mya? Your mom?" Concern filled his eyes.

"Yeah, they're fine."

He frowned. "So, spit it out."

"Mya wants to foster kids."

Jase reared back. "She wants to *what*?"

"Yeah, I know." I scrubbed my jaw.

"Like now or after college?"

"After college. You have to be at least twenty-one to get a license." Although her birthday was in a few weeks, I was pretty sure no one was going to entrust a kid's wellbeing to a college student.

"I thought she wanted to do the social work thing?"

"She does... at least, I think she still does. It kind of took me by surprise."

"Yeah, I bet." He flagged the bartender and ordered a drink. "So how do you feel about it?"

"Honestly? I don't know. I mean, I want kids. I can't wait to get her knocked up." Jase shook his head at that, and I frowned. "What?"

"We're barely twenty-one."

"I know, but I've always wanted a family."

"I'll say it again... we're *twenty-one*."

I flipped him off. "You're telling me you don't want the big house and lots of kids?"

"One day, when we're much, *much* older. I want to enjoy Felicity first. Make a life together, ya know? Besides, if I draft—"

"Which we both know you will," I smirked.

"Life will be crazy."

"Yeah, I get it." I ran my thumb over the neck of the bottle. "I told Coach I'm not looking to go pro."

He let out a long breath. "I always knew you were unsure, but I didn't think you'd made the final decision."

"It's just not what I want. I love football. I love being on the team. But I want more after college."

"Like babies?"

"Fuck off." I chuckled.

"It's a damn shame, Ash. You could have gone all the way."

"Maybe, maybe not. But I don't yearn for it the way you do. I thought maybe breaking free from my old man's expectations, I'd find my passion for it again. But honestly, it never came. I'm happy where I am. And once we graduate, I want to expand the business here. I spoke to my dad and he's going to put out some feelers."

"Well, if that's what you want then good luck to you." He lifted his beer and topped it toward me.

"It is."

"But back to the fostering thing." Jase's expression sobered. "Is it a deal breaker?"

"What? *No!*" Panic snaked through me. "I'd do anything to make Mya happy."

"Yeah, but come on, Ash. Taking on the responsibility of a kid who isn't your blood?"

"I'm not saying it would be easy, but I have money, resources... shouldn't I use them for a good cause?"

"You're a better man than me. I'm not sure I could do it."

"I'm still not convinced I can." But for Mya, I'd try. "Speaking of kids, have you spoken to Cam?"

"Yeah, he's really worried about Xander. Apparently, he's getting into some trouble at school."

"Shit." I'd known things were bad, but we hadn't talked in a few days.

"I think he'd move back to Rixon in a heartbeat if it wasn't for Hailee." Jason let out a weary sigh. "I'm worried about them."

"They'll figure it out. Xander is one of the most loved kids I know."

"Yeah." He said. But he didn't look convinced.

And maybe he was right. Maybe sometimes love wasn't enough.

"It's good to see you," I said.

I had friends at Temple. Diego, Aiden, Farrow, and the

rest of the team. But none had ever come close to filling the hole left behind by Jason and Cameron.

What we had was rare.

Special.

It was a fucking blessing.

And I thanked the universe every day for giving me two of the best friends a guy could ask for.

———

"Mya, it's so lovely to see you." Mom pulled my girl into her arms and my heart swelled watching the two of them.

They'd formed a special bond after the shooting, and it was a giant relief that the two most important women in my life got on.

"Son." Dad extended his hand and I accepted it. "It's good to see you both."

It had only been a few days since he drove out to see me, but it was the weekend before the team's first game, so we wanted to do dinner before life became too hectic to see them.

"Something smells delicious." Mom beamed.

"I slaved for hours over this, you'd better enjoy it," I teased, shooting Mya a knowing wink.

"Let me guess, sweetheart," Mom said to Mya. "You did all the heavy lifting." She chuckled.

"Ash likes to think he prepared everything, but sitting on the stool, giving me instructions on how to chop the onion—"

"Hey, I helped."

"Give up now, Son," Dad suggested, managing a rare smile.

"Fine, fine. Steal all my thunder."

"Oh, hush." Mom came over and ruffled my hair, her eyes clouded with melancholy.

She'd found it hard after everything to let me go, but she understood, perhaps better than anyone, my desire to follow Mya to Temple.

"Why don't you get your parents a drink?" Mya said, "and I'll finish up in here."

"Sure thing." I moved around Mom and went to her, pressing a kiss to her forehead. "Holler for me if you need any help."

"I think I have it handled," Mya mumbled, going back to stirring the contents of the pan.

"Come on, why don't we wait in the living room?" I got them a drink each and we made our way through the apartment. I took a seat in a chair, leaving the couch for Mom and Dad.

"How are classes?" Mom asked.

"Good."

"And the team?"

"We're looking strong. It should be a good season."

"That's great, Andy. Isn't that great?" She frowned, as my father toyed with something on the sideboard.

"Andrew?"

"What is this?" He turned slowly and my stomach sank.

Shit.

He was holding the fostering information leaflet Mya

had brought home for me to look at.

"Asher, what is this?" he repeated.

"Relax, Dad," I replied. "It's just a leaflet."

"About fostering."

"I'm sure it's nothing, Andy. Probably something to do with Mya's course. Come sit down," Mom patted the couch.

He dropped the leaflet on the side and joined us. "Tell me you're not seriously considering fostering, Son?"

"And if we were?" I sat straighter, feeling a lick of irritation up my spine.

"Be reasonable, Asher. You're just kids. You have your whole lives ahead of you to think about kids. I thought you wanted to focus on the business, on growing—"

"I do," I snapped, hating that no matter how hard he tried to be better, to do better, underneath it all, Andrew Bennet was still the same rigid, narrow-minded man he'd always been.

"Did you know that lots of young professionals foster?"

"Sweetheart, this is... well, it's a lot." Mom looked flustered. "I thought Mya wanted to graduate and do her social work training?"

"She does, but her heart is with working with kids. This is the best of both worlds."

"Now, hang on a minute, Son. It sounds like you've already made the decision. You're in junior year. There's still two years left of—"

"Hmm, is everything okay?" Mya appeared in the doorway.

"Actually," I said, standing. "I was just telling my

171

parents about the fostering thing."

"You were?" Her eyes darted to them and back to me, confusion glittering in her gaze.

"Yeah, my dad noticed the leaflet and had some questions." I gave him a tight smile.

"I see. Well, it's really only a pipe dream at the moment," she said.

"Asher made it sound like it's already decided," Dad clipped out and I heard my mom shush him.

"He did, did he?" Mya narrowed her eyes, slowly approaching me. "What are you doing?" she mouthed.

Roping my arm around her waist, I pulled her close. "I've been thinking... and I think we should do it. As soon as you turn twenty-one, we should see about getting our license and—"

"Whoa, slow down." Strangled laughter spilled from her lips. "We still have to graduate."

"I know. But I've been thinking about Xander and Hugo and all the work you do at New Hope. If we can give some kid a safe place and security and a chance at a better future, we should do it."

Deep down, I think I'd known the second Mya brought it up that it was the right move, but we were young, and it was a big decision.

I wanted it though.

I wanted it with Mya.

Her lip curved. "Yeah?"

"Yeah." I nodded. "I can start the business and you can stay at home with the kids and play Suzy Homemaker." It was my turn to smile.

Mya batted my chest. "You did not just say that."

"Oh, I did." Parents forgotten, I dipped my head, and brushed my lips over hers. "We'll need a house, something with more space and a yard; oh, and a dog. I've always wanted a dog."

"You're crazy."

"Certifiable." I grinned, but the rough bark of my father's cough, ruined the moment.

"Son, we should probably talk about this."

"Actually, Dad," I said, tucking Mya into my side. "I don't think there's anything else to talk about. We're doing this. You can either get on board with it, or not. But it won't change anything."

Not a damn thing.

Because I wasn't lying when I said I'd give Mya everything she wanted. As I stood there, with my girl by my side, and my parents watching on as if I'd lost my damn mind, a sense of peace washed over me.

And suddenly, nothing about it seemed crazy anymore.

It felt good.

It felt *right*.

It felt like things were exactly the way they were supposed to be.

Mya

"I can't believe you told your parents we're going to foster." I lifted my head off Asher's shoulder and smiled up at him.

"It just came out. He started berating me and something inside me snapped."

173

"He's just worried, they both are."

"And I get it, but I'm not a kid anymore. We're old enough to make our own decisions."

"And you definitely want this?" I stared at him with wide eyes.

"I want you to be happy, Mya. I want to make a home with you, start a family."

God, the conviction in his voice was everything. Overwhelming in the best kind of way.

Asher meant every word and it just filled me with so much emotion, I bit down gently on my lip. "You know, *if* we look into doing this, it probably means putting a baby on hold for a few years."

Why did the thought of making babies with Asher make my heart flutter?

Because he's your forever guy, your happily-ever-after.

"And that's okay. I'm in no rush for anything. I just want to know it's in the cards."

"It is. It definitely is." I relaxed back into the crook of his arm. "I think I want two kids. A boy and a girl."

"A boy and a girl and a house full of foster kids."

"I don't know about a house full." One would be enough. But ever since I'd had the idea, I couldn't get it out of my head.

"You know, there's something we probably need to discuss first." Asher slid off the couch and onto his knees in front of me. He pulled my hand into his and pressed his lips together.

"Oh my god," I breathed. "Tell me you're not about to

do what I think you're about to do?" My heart crashed violently against my ribcage.

"I think I am." His voice trembled. "I didn't plan it like this... Fuck, I don't even have a ring. But I love you, Mya. I love you so fucking much, and sitting here, talking about babies and the future... well, it's got me feeling all kinds of crazy."

"Asher, you don't need to do this... not now... not like this."

"Yeah, babe, I kind of do. Because ring or no ring, I love you and I want to spend the rest of my life loving you. You want a house full of foster kids, but I just want you, Mya. Say yes... say yes and make me the happiest guy on the planet."

"Yes," I cried, launching myself into his arms. We landed in a tangle of limbs and laughter.

"Yes?" Asher stared up at me, and I grinned.

"Yes, I'll marry you, you crazy idiot."

"Oh fuck, did I really just do that?" The blood drained from his face. "I can't believe I did that. I don't even have a ring for fuck's sake."

"Asher, look at me." I gripped his jaw. "I don't need a ring. I don't need a romantic gesture or a huge public display of affection. I only need this." My other hand went to his breastbone, right where his heart lay.

"Yeah?" His voice was small.

"Yeah."

"Good." His expression morphed into pure joy. "Because I'm not taking it back ever. You're mine now, Mya Hernandez, and I'm never letting you go."

17

Asher

"Hold on, I'm just connecting Cam now."

"Ash? What is it?" Cameron's face appeared on the screen.

"Can you see us?" I asked, and he nodded. "Jason and Fee too?"

Another nod.

"Okay." I took a deep breath, hugging Mya to my side. "We have something to tell you..."

"Oh my god, you didn't?" Felicity shrieked, clutching Jase's shoulder.

"We did," Mya said, shooting me an infectious smile. "We're engaged."

"Congratulations," Hailee and Cameron said.

"Nice one," Jase grinned, and Fee blurted out, "Let's see it then."

"Well, I... so, funny story..."

"Asher Bennet," she groaned. "Please tell me you didn't propose without a ring."

"It just sort of happened."

"Oh shit," Jase breathed. "You didn't get a ring."

"Hang on a second, it isn't like that," I argued, and Mya buried her face into my neck, smothering her laughter.

"Ash, I was counting on you for the grand romantic gesture," Felicity let out an exasperated breath.

"I think it's sweet," Hailee added. "Spur of the moment. I like that."

"Back up, Giles," Jase was no longer looking at us. Instead, his eyes were fixed on his fiancée. "What the fuck is that supposed to mean? I made a big gesture. Or have you forgotten when I got down on one knee on *national television*?"

"Don't be silly, babe, I haven't forgotten, and it was very sweet, but I had high hopes for Asher and Mya."

"Guys," I interrupted. "It's not like I don't plan on getting a ring. We're going shopping in the week to look—"

"No, no, no." Fee looked mortified. "You can't let Mya pick her own ring, it's bad luck."

"Well, I'm glad we decided to call our *friends* and share our happy news with them."

"Ignore them," Hailee said. "I think it's great news. I'm so happy for you both."

"Thank you." Mya leaned her head on my shoulder.

"Have you talked about wedding plans yet?"

"Seriously?" I balked. "I didn't even get a ring..."

Mya dug her fingers into my ribs, and I yelped. "No, we haven't," she said. "Sometime after graduation. We're in no rush."

"You're the last man standing now, Cam," I smirked. "You know that, right? It's time you upped your game."

"Ash..." Hailee warned.

"Relax, he knows I'm joking."

"Trust me, when I do finally pop the question, I'll make sure to have an actual ring."

"Burn," Jason hissed, unable to hide his amusement.

"Okay, this has been nice and all, but I want some alone time with my fiancée."

"Not until you put a ring on—"

I hit end call and dropped my cell on the counter, pulling Mya around to me.

"Ash, that was rude."

"Nah, they get it." Cameron and Jason were as infatuated with their girlfriends as I was with Mya. They understood what it was like to want to bury yourself so deep inside her, you didn't know where you ended, and she began.

"I need you, Mya." Heat coursed through my veins.

"Well, I'm right here." She licked her lips.

I prowled toward her and ran my hand along the curve of her neck. "Mine," I breathed.

Mya's breath caught, her eyes fluttering closed. "Is this real life?" she whispered.

"Does this feel like real life?" I asked her, leaning in to swipe my tongue over her salty sweet skin.

She reached for me, curling her hands into my Temple U hoodie. Without warning, I slipped my hands to the backs of Mya's thighs and hoisted her against me. Her legs wound around my hips and she shrieked with surprise. Spinning us around, I dropped her on the counter and pushed myself between her thighs. "I love you, Mya. Today, tomorrow, and all the days after."

"Show me..."

Oh, I would.

I intended on showing her all night long.

Mya

"Hey, Mya," Sally looked up from her desk. "The boys are running late."

"Everything okay?" I frowned.

"I think Hugo had a bad day at school. Mariah said some kids have been giving him a hard time."

"They're six."

"I know, right? Kids can be so cruel. But hopefully seeing you will cheer him up."

"Oh, I don't know about that."

"Hey, none of that. You're making a difference, Mya. You just have to trust the process. Be there. Show up. These kids need to learn to trust adults again."

"You're right." I nodded.

"And who knows, maybe today will the day he decides to use his words."

But it wasn't.

As soon as Hugo and his brothers arrived at the center, it was apparent that whatever had gone down had made him even less willing to engage.

But I wouldn't quit. I would be patient. I would wait. And eventually—*hopefully*—I would help.

———

Another week passed, and I was no closer to getting Hugo to open up to me.

I knew not to take it personally; it wasn't about me. It was about the little boy with eyes the color of honey, clinging onto the stuffed Eagle as if it was his life raft.

While he sank further into himself, his brothers flourished in their new foster home and sessions with Pat and Hershel. Jay liked football, basketball, dodgeball; any sport that involved a ball really. Although Mario enjoyed sport, he was also super creative. He and Hershel had started painting a mural on one of the walls inside the main hall. For a fourteen-year-old, the kid oozed talent. When it was finished, I was hoping to invite Hailee down for the unveiling. I knew she'd have something to say to Mario about it.

"Hey, buddy," I said, sliding onto the bench beside Hugo. "How was your week so far?"

Silence stretched before us as he half-heartedly colored in another printout of Swoop.

"So, remember my boyfriend, Asher? The football player? Well, it's his first game tomorrow."

A flicker of interest flashed across Hugo's face, but he didn't meet my gaze. "The Owls play at the Lincoln Financial Field too, but I bet you already knew that."

More silence. I ran a hand down my face, racking my brain for something, *anything*, that might get Hugo engaging with me. Sally caught my eye across the room and gave me a reassuring smile. A smile that said I was doing the right thing, no matter how useless I felt.

But Hugo didn't engage. He didn't smile or gaze up at

me, eager for my tidbits about Asher and the team. He just sat there, coloring in and clutching his stuffed toy as if I wasn't even there.

By the time the session was over, I was emotionally weary. Asher was picking me up and we were going to watch a movie, so once I'd helped clean up, I grabbed my purse out of the locker in the staff room and headed out.

"Bye, guys," I said to Pat and Hershel. They gave me a quick wave and I made a beeline for the door.

Asher met me halfway. "Hey, how was it?"

I shook my head, noticing Sally waiting with the Garcia kids.

"Is that your boyfriend?" Jay called over.

"Jay," Sally warned.

"It's okay," I said, approaching them. "This is Asher, my boyfriend." My lips curved, as I discreetly watched Hugo. He peered up at Asher and then my fiancé did the most incredible thing. He crouched low and held up a fist.

"Hey, you must be Hugo. Mya has told me all about you. She said you want to be just like Fletcher Cox when you're older?"

Jay and Mario could barely contain their excitement, but not Hugo. He simply stared up at Asher, his eyes wide and lips parted.

"Is that Swoop?" Asher asked, completely unfazed at Hugo's lack of reply. "Can I see him?" He slowly extended his hand but didn't get too close.

"Asher," I whispered, not wanting him to scare Hugo. But then slowly, Hugo pushed Swoop forward and placed him in Asher's open palm.

"He looks like he could do with a bath."

Hugo smiled. It was only small, full of trepidation and uncertainty.

But it was a smile.

I looked up at Sally and I knew the emotion in her eyes mirrored the emotion in mine.

"Did Mya tell you it's our first game of the season tomorrow?"

Hugo nodded.

This was freaking huge. I'd spent weeks trying to get the little boy with pain in his eyes to engage with me, and Asher had managed to do it in under a minute.

"I'm going to ask our running back to score a touchdown just for you." Asher handed Swoop back and held up his fist again. "What do you say?"

Hugo made a small fist and bumped it to Asher's. "Awesome. Mya can let you know next time how we got on, okay?" He stood up. "What about you two, you like football?"

Jay pulled up to his full height and puffed out his chest. "Hell yeah." Sally cleared her throat and he murmured, "I mean, sure do."

"What's your name, kid?"

"Jay, and this is my brother Mario."

"Well, it was nice to meet you all. Perhaps I can drop by with a few guys from the team one day and we can hang out?" I nudged him, and he added, "If Sally says it's okay." He shot my mentor a blinding smile.

"I'm sure we can figure something out," she said returning it with her own.

"You three be good, okay? And I'll see you soon." Asher took my hand and guided me away, the sounds of Jay and Mario's excited chatter following us.

"I can't believe you just did that. You were so good with him."

"Nah." Asher gave me a coy look. "I didn't do anything, not really."

"You did. Hugo hasn't responded to anyone at the center like that, or his foster parents. It was... wow."

I couldn't even be envious that Asher had made the breakthrough with Hugo I so desperately wanted, because seeing the guy I loved interact so easily with the lost little boy had been nothing short of heart melting.

"I think I just fell in love with you all over again."

We reached Asher's Jeep and he pulled me into his arms. "He's a cute kid. I can see why he's got you all tied up in knots."

"I just want to reach him, ya know?"

"I know." He leaned in, kissing me softly. "I meant what I said. Me and the guys will drop by one session and play some ball with them. I don't know why we've never thought of it before. Maybe we could get a regular thing going. Coach would love that, having the team giving back to the community."

"That would be... the kids would love that." The other volunteers too no doubt. "You're really okay with this, aren't you?"

"With what?" His brows bunched together.

"The fostering thing... the work I do."

"Mya, I don't know how to make this any clearer to you,

but I will always, *always* support your dreams. I fell for your spirit, your passion and drive... your big heart. I'm crazy in love with you, Mya Hernandez, and one day I'm going to put a huge ring on your finger and claim you as mine in front of all our friends, family, and our houseful of foster kids."

"I'd like that."

"Good, because it's happening, Mya. We just gotta finish school first." Asher gazed at me with such reverence it took my breath away.

There had been a time when I had questioned what I'd done to deserve Asher, but I realized now it wasn't about being deserving. Our souls were the same. We loved hard and we fought hard for those we cared about. *That's* what brought us together, and that's what would set the foundation of our life together.

And I couldn't wait.

18

Mya

"That's quite the man you have," Sally said when I arrived at New Hope on the Monday after Asher's first game.

"Yeah, he's really something."

"Gosh, I remember that feeling," she sighed. "To be so in love it radiates from your pores." She grinned.

"Crap." I blushed. "I've become *that* girl, haven't I?"

"Yeah, hon, I think you have. But it seems Asher worked his magic because I spoke to Mariah earlier and they had a really good weekend with Hugo."

"He spoke to them?"

"No." Her expression fell a little. "But he was using non-verbal cues and even joined in some of their activities."

"That's amazing."

"I have a good feeling about this, Mya."

I left Sally to her paperwork and made my way into the main hall. I instantly saw the difference in Hugo. He was no longer huddled at one of the tables, clutching his stuffed eagle. Instead, he was on the fringe of the game. He wasn't exactly participating, but he wasn't *not* participating either.

Smiling to myself, I made my way over to him and crouched down. "Hey, buddy. You want to join in?"

He shrugged.

"Maybe there's something else you'd like to do?" He slid his small hand into mine and my heart swelled. Hugo led me over to his usual table and helped himself to a sheet of paper and a crayon, scribbling something. He thrust the paper at me, and I read it aloud.

"Did they win? The Owls?" I smiled, and he nodded. "They sure did, buddy. The running back scored two touchdowns just for you."

His whole face lit up.

"In fact, I have a photo. Asher asked me to show it to you." I dug it out of my pocket and passed it to him. We'd gone to the mall and had it printed out so Hugo could keep it. It was a shot of Asher and the Owls' running back, Aiden, celebrating. They were pointing right at the camera, right at Hugo.

His smile grew.

"You can keep that. See, Asher and some of team signed the back for you." His little fingers clutched the photograph as if it was the most precious thing he'd ever received.

"Remember your envelope is waiting. Whenever you're ready," I said.

I didn't push. It had to be on Hugo's terms, if ever. But he'd made such a huge step and it was all thanks to my fiancé.

God, I would never tire of saying that.

At least, until he was my husband.

I swallowed down the rush of emotion. Something brushed my hand and I looked down to find Hugo tugging my fingers.

"What's up, buddy?" He beckoned me down to him, so I crouched down to meet his eye level.

Tentatively, he leaned in, cupping his hands around his mouth. "O- open envelope please," he said.

"Yeah?" My heart almost burst.

He nodded, looking skittish. I didn't want to scare him off, so I steeled myself and kept an even tone. "That's really great to hear, Hugo. Shall we go get it down?"

"Yes, please." His voice was barely a whisper, but his words were perfect.

I stood and held out my hand. Hugo took it, and everyone in the center stopped to watch as we crossed the room and I plucked the envelope off the shelf, handing it to him.

"Go ahead, open it," I said. "And then we can see if we can make your wish come true."

Asher

"Stop," Diego grunted. "You're like a fucking yo-yo."

"I'm just nervous."

"Dude, it's a bunch of kids. What could possibly go wrong?"

Diego had clearly never met some of the kids Mya worked with. They wouldn't hesitate to tell us if what we had planned was totally lame and uncool. But hopefully they would all enjoy it.

Especially Hugo.

Mya had come home that day—the day he finally chose to use his words—a teary-eyed emotional mess. I'd held her while she cried her happy tears and then she'd given me a blow-by-blow account of what had happened.

The little guy had done amazing, so it was only right he got to see his wish come true. Coach had been able to pull a few strings, and together, he and Sally had arranged the event at the football field today.

"They're here." I spotted Mya and Sally and a handful of the other volunteers walking out of the tunnel with Hugo, his brothers, and some of the other kids in New Hope's program for kids in the foster care system.

They were wide-eyed, their expressions full of wonder as they took in the vastness of the Lincoln Financial Field stadium.

"Come on," I said to the guys. "Let's go introduce ourselves. And remember, keep cussing to a minimum."

"Yeah, yeah, Bennet, keep your hair on. I think we can behave for an hour." Aiden chuckled.

"Hey." Mya reached us. We were here on official team business, but it didn't stop me leaning in to press a chaste kiss to her cheek. "They're so excited," she whispered.

"How are you all doing?" I asked the huddle of kids. Jay and Mario were grinning ear to ear, but most of the other kids looked like Hugo, completely awestruck.

"You ready to play some ball with us?"

A chorus of 'yeahs' filled the air. "Well, before we get started with some warm-up activities, I have a little surprise for you. Bring him out, Coach," I yelled.

"You did it," Mya breathed, reaching my hand, as we watched Swoop the eagle traipse out onto the field.

Hugo clapped his hands with glee, and I crouched down to his level. "What do you think, buddy?"

He looked at me with tears shining in his eyes, and whispered, "Best. Day. Ever."

Mya

"Hey guys, over here." Faith beckoned us over to where she and Rex were sitting. "We didn't think you were going to make it."

"We almost didn't," Asher murmured, and I elbowed him in the ribs.

"Play nice," I mouthed.

When Faith had called to ask if Asher and I would meet her for drinks, I'd almost told her no. Things between us were okay, but I'd had no intentions of putting her and Asher in a room together anytime soon. But he'd overheard the call and said everyone deserved a second chance. So here we were, meeting Faith and... Rex, for drinks.

Odd, she hadn't mentioned him in her original invitation.

"I hear congratulations are in order," Rex said to Asher.

"Yeah, thanks."

"Listen, I hope there are no hard feelings about before. You guys are perfect for each other, and I was being a judgmental bastard."

"No hard feelings." Asher squeezed my hand under the table, his touch lingering on my finger.

We still hadn't picked out a ring, but honestly, I didn't need one. I had everything I could ever want. We were engaged, I turned twenty-one soon, and things at the center were going great since Asher got the team involved.

The session that day had gone so well, both Coach Johnson and Sally had wanted to make it a regular thing. She was currently looking at setting up the infrastructure to make it a permanent feature of the center's program.

It had been such a great day, watching the kids interact and bond with the team. Hugo had followed Asher around like a lost puppy and the two of them had become fast friends. So much so, that Asher had signed up for the program's in-house training sessions so he could be an official volunteer.

Life was good.

Perfect, even.

We'd celebrated our engagement over the weekend back in Rixon. Asher's mom had invited my aunt for dinner and the five of us enjoyed good food and easy conversation, the tension of our past staying right where it belonged. Even Asher's dad had managed to congratulate us, hugging me tight and telling me that the wedding was taken care of; all we had to do was let him know what we wanted.

But I didn't want a big fanfare. All I needed was something small with the people I cared about most in the world.

"I like this place," I said, glancing around the coffee shop Faith had picked. "It has character."

"Right? We come here a lot."

"You do?" I frowned, glancing between her and Rex. Guilt shone in Faith's eyes.

"Actually, that's why I asked you to come. There's something I have to tell you... and I don't want it to be weird, all right? But you're one of my best friends and I know I was a total bitch at the beginning of the semester—"

"Faith take a breath. What is going on?"

"Oh, Boo Boo, just spit it out already. She isn't going to care."

Boo Boo? What the hell?

Asher almost choked on his coffee.

"Me and Rex, well, we're—"

"Together. We're together, okay?" He huffed dramatically. "Good. Now we can all move on with life."

"I'm sorry, can we just back up a second, to the part where you just said the two of you are..."

"*Together?*" Rex smirked.

"I did not see that coming." Asher let out a low whistle and I nudged him again.

"I know, I know." Faith buried her face in her hands. "I'm a complete hypocrite."

"How long has this been going on?" I asked.

"Officially, a couple of weeks."

"And unofficially?"

"We were fucking most of the summer."

"*Rex!*" Faith hissed.

"So the summer of sexual inhibition and self-discovery was—"

"I lied. And I feel like a horrible person. But things

191

with Rex were confusing and I didn't want to jump headfirst from one relationship into another. God, you must think I'm such a bitch."

"Faith, stop." I sighed. "Are you happy?"

"Yeah, I mean... it's new and unexpected. But Rex is so different to Max."

"Well, duh." He grinned, sliding his arm around her shoulder.

"I'm sorry, but I don't see it, at all," Asher said.

"That makes two of us," Faith offered him an uncertain smile. "But the heart wants what the hearts want, am I right? Listen, I really am sorry about everything I said to Mya."

"She's forgiven you," he said, "so I guess that makes us cool."

"As long as you're happy," I added, "what me or anyone else thinks shouldn't matter."

"You're right, it shouldn't. But I don't always find it easy to shake people's expectations."

"You'll get there, Boo Boo." Rex nuzzled her neck, and I sat there watching, completely bewildered. They were so... different. Faith was all about appearances and what other people thought, and Rex was... Rex. He didn't really conform to gender stereotypes or label himself as straight or gay.

It was weird... but even weirder was the fact that as I watched them whisper to one another, wrapped up in their own little bubble, it didn't seem weird at all.

"Well, I don't know about anyone else," Asher said. "But I'm really glad we cleared the air."

My friends chuckled, and I smiled, a strange sensation washing over me.

I'd been Faith once upon a time. A girl lost and unsure of her place in the world, wanting to break free from the stereotypes forced on her. Then I'd found Asher and he'd taught me love had no limits. It was hard and messy and chaotic, but worth the fight and the tears and the heartache.

Love was what made us human.

But how someone else loved us made us feel more than human.

And Asher...

He loved me enough to make me feel like the luckiest girl in the world.

PART III

Senior Year

19

Cameron

"Chase, a word?" Coach beckoned me toward his office, and I weaved my way through the locker room. The air was warm, the smell of sweaty cleats and wet grass lingering.

Practice had been grueling, and I knew Coach Byford probably wanted to know where my head was at.

"Hey, Coach."

"Take a seat, son." He motioned to the seat opposite his desk and I sat. "Do I need to be worried?" Fingers steepled, he sat back, studying me.

"It's my brother, sir. He's..." Fuck. I didn't know what the hell was going on with Xander. He'd only been in second grade a few weeks and my parents had already been called in four times.

Four.

"He's finding it tough."

Coach whipped off his ball cap and let out a long breath. "That's rough, Cameron. I feel for the little fella, I do. But this is your senior year, son, and the team have a real shot at going all the way. I need to know my best wide receiver has his head on straight."

"I know, Coach. I'm sorry."

"You're a good brother, Cam, and you're a good guy. But the team needs you, here, on the field."

I nodded, unable to reply over the lump in my throat.

"Scouts are going to be making the rounds soon enough, and you've got it, son. But you need to leave all the other crap at the door, okay? When you come into my locker room, you come with a clear head and—"

"And hunger for the win."

"Damn straight. Now get out of here."

I got up and made for the door, but Coach's voice stopped me at the last second. "And Chase?"

"Yes, sir?"

"You ever need to talk, my door is always open."

"Thanks, Coach." I gave him a small nod before slipping back into the locker room. My quarterback, a guy called Dominic Sanchez, was waiting.

"Everything good?"

"He's worried." My lips pursed.

"Does he need to be worried?"

"I'll be okay."

He clapped me on the back. "Do you know what I think you need?"

"No, but I'm sure you're going to enlighten me."

Dom guided me over to our corner of the benches. "You need to go find that woman of yours and let her help relieve all the tension you got going on, if you know what I'm saying."

"Amen to that, brother." Dylan, our running back, held his hand out and the two of them fist bumped.

"Beats hanging around with you bunch of losers." I shot back around a smirk. But it was all front.

It had been for a while.

I loved my team. I loved my classes and living in Michigan with Hailee.

But I didn't love being four-hundred miles from home, from my kid brother and his struggles.

Everyone—Mom, Dad, Jase and Asher, even Hailee—kept telling me it was only eight more months. Eight more months until we could move back to Rixon and be closer to my family. But I couldn't shake the pit in my stomach, the feeling that this was only the beginning, that Xander knew something the rest of us didn't.

And that terrified the shit out of me.

———

"Hailee?" I threw my keys on the sideboard and moved deeper into our loft apartment overlooking the Huron River.

The chilled beats of Röyksopp drifted down the hall and I knew exactly where to find her. Grabbing a beer from the refrigerator, I kicked off my sneakers and headed for the mezzanine. Sure enough, Hailee was standing over a canvas with her back to me, paintbrush in hand.

I leaned against the wall for a second, drinking in the sight of her. While I'd found it hard being away from Rixon —from my family—Hailee had flourished at Michigan. She loved every second of her arts degree and her talent had grown substantially. So much so that last spring we'd decided to get a bigger place, somewhere to accommodate her growing collection of paintings and sculptures.

Our new place was perfect. It was an industrial warehouse that had been converted into huge open plan apartments. Ours was lucky enough to have a mezzanine that was perfect for Hailee's studio, without her feeling locked away in a different part of the apartment.

Her body swayed gently to the music as she brushed long sweeping arcs over the splodges of color already decorating the canvas. Almost four years later, and I still didn't really understand most of her art. But I loved watching her. Her work attire didn't hurt the eyes either.

She currently stood in an oversized white shirt that grazed her thighs. Hailee had pulled her hair into a loose bun at the nape of her neck, and from the way the shirt was hanging off one shoulder, I knew she'd probably left some buttons open.

Taking a long pull on my beer, I placed it on the sideboard and quietly moved closer. She was too lost in her art to notice me. Or, at least, I was thought she was, until she said, "How long were you watching me?"

"Busted." I smiled, brushing the stray hairs off her neck and leaning in to press a kiss there.

A shudder rolled through her, and Hailee glanced back at me. "What is it? What's wrong?"

Her words wrapped around me like a warm blanket. She knew. Hailee always knew when something was wrong, but I tried my best to make sure she didn't know just how much I was struggling. I didn't want to be a burden, not on her. Not when she'd worked so hard to get here.

Studying at STAMPS art and design school had always been her dream, and I'd be damned if I did anything to ruin that.

Besides, it was only eight more months.

"Practice was tough."

Her brows furrowed. "Let me finish up here and we can—"

"Is it an important piece?" I flicked my gaze to the canvas.

"Just something for me."

Thank fuck.

I pulled the brush from her fingers and threw it down on the tray.

"Cameron, what are you—"

My fingers slid to her neck, my thumbs smoothing over her soft skin. Hailee's breath caught. "That bad, huh?" Her eyes darkened.

"It was pretty bad." I'd fumbled the ball, barely caught Dom's passes, and defense had taken me down seven out of ten plays.

It was a fucking shit show.

"I'm sorry." She fisted my hoodie, anchoring us together. "What do you need?"

"You," I breathed against her lips. "I only need you."

Hailee

I felt Cameron's torment as he kissed me. I knew he was worried about Xander; it had gotten worse every year that we were away from Rixon. He constantly reassured me he was okay, that he wanted to graduate from Michigan before we decided what to do *after*, but it was taking its toll.

His tongue slipped past my lips, curling around mine. Cameron kissed the way he played ball, sure and steady and in complete control. And it wasn't long before our hands were searching for skin, desperate to touch and explore.

"This needs to go," he said between kisses, fingering the buttons of my work shirt.

"Here, let me." I broke away, helping him undo the buttons, baring myself to him.

More often than not, I painted in just a shirt. I liked the freedom and it saved on laundry.

Cam dipped his head, kissing the curve of my breasts as he backed me against the wall.

"We could take this downstairs," I suggested. It was a mess up here.

"No," he breathed. "I need you, Hailee." His fingers went to his sweats, pushing them down his hips right along with his boxers. His hoodie and t-shirt went next until he was standing in front of me stark naked.

God, he was beautiful. Strong and stacked, his torso was a solid slab of muscle, each ab perfectly chiseled and defined.

I reached for him, trailing my hand over the cherry blossom snaking up his arm. Next, I traced the tattoo he'd gotten of the artwork I'd painted on him with my own hand in senior year. It was our initials—HR and CC—looped together with a delicate heart over his pec.

"What?" he asked, his voice a hushed whisper.

"I love you, Cameron." *So much it scares me.*

He crowded me against the wall and picked me up, pressing my back against the bare brick. "Not as much as I love you." He grasped himself and lined himself up with my center, pressing into me.

"Oh God," I moaned as I sank down on him.

Cameron stilled, touching his head to mine and taking a shuddering breath.

"It's okay." I laid a hand on his cheek. "I'm here, Cameron, I'm right here."

Burying his face in my neck, he pulled out slowly before thrusting back inside. It was deep like this, intense and overwhelming in the best kind of way.

"Harder," I said, letting my head fall back. "Take what you need."

Cam squeezed my hip, hard enough to leave a bruise as he rocked into me over and over. "Fuck, Sunshine," he groaned. "You feel like heaven."

He attacked my mouth like a man starved, all tongue and teeth and teasing strokes.

"Cameron..." His name was a breathy plea on my lips as I drowned in sensation.

"Feel me, Hailee." *Thrust.* "Feel what you do to me." *Thrust.* "Nothing... *nothing* will ever feel as good as this."

He went harder... faster... *deeper*, driving me into the wall until I knew I'd have friction burns. But it didn't matter. Cameron needed this and I wanted to be the one to give it to him.

Only ever me.

"I love you," he panted against my damp skin. "I love

you so fucking much." Cameron kissed my throat, licking and sucking, branding me with his lips and searing me with his touch.

"Harder," I cried, clinging onto Cam's broad shoulders for dear life as he pushed me toward the precipice of sheer bliss.

"Fuck, Hailee." He slammed inside me, once, twice... until I shattered around him, crying his name over and over.

Cameron stilled, riding his own waves of pleasure. He gathered me into his arms and just held me.

"It's okay," I whispered against the corner of his mouth. "It's going to be okay."

But as I said the words, I knew it was a lie.

Because this was one thing I didn't know how to fix.

Cameron

"Come here," I patted the bed and Hailee climbed in beside me. After we'd cleaned up, she had reheated some leftovers and we'd eaten together before calling it a night.

I was weary from practice and Hailee was tired from the way I'd used her body against the wall.

"How are you feeling?" she asked me.

"I'm just worried about him."

"I know. But you can't fix everything, Cam."

I couldn't, I knew that. But if I was there, if Xan had me there to talk to, to distract him...

Fuck.

Guilt chewed me up inside. He was my kid brother.

My little shadow. He was lost and no one knew how to help him.

"They're coming to the game Friday?"

"Yeah, Dad booked them into the hotel on Denton Avenue."

"I'm sure seeing you will cheer him up."

"Yeah." He usually perked up whenever I went home or he visited us, but as he'd gotten older, he'd started to pull away. Although I knew it was irrational, I couldn't deny it felt like he was punishing me.

"Can I ask you something?" Hailee sat up, and I nodded. "Do you ever regret coming to Michigan with me?"

"What? *No!* Hailee, that's not—"

"I'm not trying to make you feel guilty, I'm not." She gave me an uncertain smile. "I'm just trying to understand how I can help. It's senior year. I don't want you to spend our last year here together resenting me."

"Hailee, stop." I cupped her face, stroking her cheek. "I don't ever want you to feel that way."

"So, you're happy here?"

"I..." I couldn't do it. I couldn't lie to her, not when she'd been there every step of the way.

"I can't help but wonder if he'd be this way if I'd have stayed." The words were like a sheet of ice between us and I instantly regretted them.

"You never said anything." Her voice cracked. "All this time and you never—"

"I didn't want you to think I didn't want to be here. I

do, so much. But he's my brother, and he isn't getting better, he's getting worse."

"So, what do we do?" Her eyes filled with tears and I hated that I was the one to put them there. But this conversation was long overdue.

Over the last couple of years, Xander had become the elephant in the room. But I constantly reassured her this was what I wanted. Because it had been.

When my mom got sick, Hailee had stood by me through the hardest few weeks of my life. I wanted to come to Michigan for her, to put her first. But now I was stuck between a rock and a hard place. Xander was family, my blood, and everything in me was screaming at me that he needed me... but Hailee, she was my heart, my home.

How the fuck was I supposed to choose between them?

The answer was, I couldn't.

20

Cameron

"Cameron." Xander shot at me like a bull out of a gate and I opened my arms catching him.

"Hey, Xan, it's good to see you." He clung to me like a spider monkey, so I slid my arms under his butt and carried him into our building.

"How's school?"

"Ugh. Don't ask. I hate that place."

"No way? Don't you have Mr. Gellar? I remember that guy, he was always a hoot."

"Well, he's a real asshat now."

"Hey, watch it," I scolded him, and he grumbled, "Sorry, Cam."

Hailee and my parents trailed in behind us, and I lowered my brother to the floor to greet them properly.

"Son, it's good to see you." Dad stepped forward and pulled me into his arms. I could see the worry lines around his eyes, but they were no longer because of mom. Instead they were caused by the seven-year-old currently drilling holes into the side of my head.

"Hey, Dad."

"Cameron," Mom nudged her way between us, looking

up at me with weary eyes. "Has it really only been a few weeks?"

"Yeah." I chuckled, but it was strained.

"And Hailee," Mom went to my girl. "You get more beautiful every time I see you."

"Thanks, Karen."

"Excited for the game tonight?" Dad asked.

"Yeah, but I'll not be excited about spending the day with this little squirt tomorrow." I tackle hugged Xander, and his laughter was like music to my ears.

"Oh, Clarke, look."

Xander instantly stiffened at Mom's words. "Relax," I said. "She's just happy—"

"Yeah, whatever." He shirked me off and went and sat on the couch. We all watched him, silence descending over the four of us.

"Why don't I make some coffee?" Hailee suggested, giving me a reassuring smile.

"Thanks," I said, sliding my eyes back to Xander. He'd pulled out his handheld computer game, his thumbs working overtime as he pressed the buttons.

"How is he, really?" I asked my parents and their expressions fell.

"We don't know what to do anymore, Cameron. He's completely shut us out."

"I'll talk to him." I ran a hand through my hair, releasing a heavy sigh. But as I watched my brother, one of the most important people in my life, I feared talking wasn't enough anymore.

Hailee

"Are you excited to watch Cameron?" I asked Xander as we sat in our seats. It was the opening game of the season, and a big rivalry game against Ohio State, so the atmosphere in the Michigan Stadium was electric.

Karen and Clarke sat on the other side of Xander, giving the two of us some space. I'd noticed how strained things were between them and their son, and my heart ached for them all.

He shrugged, and I nudged his shoulder. "It's okay to be excited, you know. But if you're not, that's okay too."

"I just really miss him," he admitted.

"He misses you too. So much. He talks about you all the time."

"He does?" He stared up at me with big blue eyes, just like his brother's.

"Yeah. Cameron loves you so much, Xander."

"But he left." His lip quivered, but he steeled his expression.

For a seven-year-old, Xander Chase had excellent resolve. It's why his mom and dad struggled so much to get him to open up to them.

"You know Cameron leaving had nothing to do with you, don't you?"

He shrugged again, just as the team jogged out onto the field. The noise was deafening and Xander seemed to shrink into his chair. He leaned into me as if he needed the protection, but he didn't get too close.

My heart swelled with pride at seeing Cameron in his maize and blue jersey.

When they had found out his mom was sick, he'd been prepared to give up his dream of football. But, in the end, he hadn't had to. His parents were so proud of him and everything he'd achieved so far at Michigan. But senior year was his year.

At least, I hoped it was.

"They're looking good," Clarke yelled over the chorus of cheers and chatter. "Strong."

"It's their year." I grinned at him.

"I really hope so."

Xander peeked up at me and I frowned. "What?"

"Are you and my brother going to get married one day?"

"I..." I stuttered over the words. "Maybe. I mean, I hope so."

Karen and Clarke smothered their laughter.

"Why?"

Please don't say you don't want us to. My heart galloped in my chest as he stared up at me before beckoning me closer. I dipped my head and waited.

"Maybe if you do, and you come back to Rixon, I can come live with you."

Oh God.

My heart.

It broke for the boy looking at me with nothing but hope and sadness in his eyes.

It broke for his parents, trying so hard to be unaffected by their son's growing detachment.

But most of all it broke because I couldn't give him the answer he thought he wanted to hear.

"Hailee?" he said.

"Uh, it's not something I can really answer, buddy."

Disappointment flashed in his eyes.

"We still have to get through college and then figure out what we want to do."

"You'll be coming home though, right?"

Crap.

This was not going well.

I was digging a deeper and deeper hole. I glanced over at Karen, but she and Clarke were deep in conversation.

"Wherever we decide to settle down, you will always be welcome, Xander." I chose my words carefully. "If we get a place big enough, you can even have your own room. We can decorate and—"

The announcer's voice came over the speaker and relief flooded me.

I gave Xander a reassuring smile, but he barely returned it, and I hoped the game would be enough to take his mind off things.

Cameron

"Okay, listen up and listen good, ladies," Coach said, his eyes glancing to the scoreboard. We were tied with a little over a minute on the clock. "We've got a shot at one final play, and we need to make it a good one. Because anything less is not an option, you hear me?"

"Yes, sir."

"Good. Now get out there and show them why that championship is coming home this season."

"Dom, take it away, son."

"Hands in," he yelled, and we all piled our hands in the center.

It had been a brutal game, our teams matched in speed, strength, and grit. But with Hailee and my family in the audience, I'd found my flow, scoring touchdowns on five out of seven passes. The only problem was Ohio had also scored.

"Wolverines on three."

"One... two... three... Wolverines." We broke from the huddle and Dom jogged beside me. "You ready?"

I gave him a stiff nod.

He curled his hand around my neck and pulled me into him, our helmets crashing together. "We've earned this, Chase. It's senior year and that championship is ours, you hear me?"

Adrenaline pulsed through me, the roar of the crowd like liquid ecstasy coursing through my veins.

When I was out here, on the field with my team, playing to the cheers of over one-hundred thousand fans, it was easy to forget about all the other shit. Xander. Hailee. My future. Decisions I wasn't sure I was ready to make.

Out here, it all went away until there was nothing but me, the ball, and a line of defensive players all looking to stop me from reaching my destination.

I knew it wouldn't last though. When the final whistle sounded, and the noise stopped, it would all come rushing back.

But for now, I was invincible.

"Let's give them a show," I called to Dom and he grinned.

"What are you thinking?"

"Remember when we were goofing around with Dylan the other day?

"Yeah?"

I nodded.

"It's a big risk."

"We can pull it off."

"Let's do it then." He jogged off toward Dylan to give him the instructions as the rest of us moved into position.

The crowd quieted as we waited for the clock to resume. If we wanted to score, we needed to move fast and execute the play to the letter.

"Blue twenty-two," Dom yelled. "Blue twenty-two." A couple of players dropped back, and the offensive line began shuffling, trying to read the play.

I stayed light on my feet waiting for the snap to Dom. He caught it and hiked the ball to Dylan who began charging for the line of scrimmage, only to slow at the line and pass back to Dominic. The offense scrambled and I flew. Pumping my legs hard, I moved into the open space, extending my hand to give him the signal. The ball cut through the air and I leaped, curling my hand around the leather. The confused Ohio players immediately switched direction to close in around me. But I was too fast, cool air whipping through my helmet as I push harder... *faster*... nothing but the end zone and victory in sight.

Fingers grazed my shoulder as a defense player reached

me, but I shirked him off, dodging right and straight into the end zone.

"Touchdooooown," the announcer's voice rang out through the stadium, the collective hoots and hollers of the tens of thousands of fans deafening.

My team jogged over, all wanting to celebrate our first win of the season against one of our biggest rivals.

"That's how you get shit done," Dom said, smashing his helmet to mine. "Fuck, I could kiss you."

"Please don't," I chuckled, trying desperately to hold onto the high. But no sooner had it arrived than it started to dissipate.

Xander was out there somewhere with my parents. They would look to me for answers, answers I didn't have.

"Get over here," Coach yelled, and we all jogged toward him. "What the hell was that, Sanchez?"

"That was getting the job done, sir."

"That flea flicker your idea, son?"

"The credit is all Chase's, sir."

Coach set his eyes in my direction. "Risky move."

"Knew we could do it, sir," I said, feeling the weight of the shoulder pads start to crush my lungs.

I needed to get off this field, and fast.

"Lucky for you, it worked."

I went to move around him, but Coach caught my arm, and I glanced back. "You played well out there tonight, son. Keep it up and you'll have nothing to worry about when the scouts come around."

His words only made my chest tighter. "Thanks, Coach," I mumbled, before tearing off my helmet and jogging toward the tunnel. I needed a shower and then I needed to find the one person who could make it all go away.

———

Not even an hour later, I filed out of the stadium to find Hailee, Xander, and my parents waiting for me.

"Congratulations." My girl rushed into my arms and wrapped herself around me. "You were amazing."

"I don't feel so amazing. Their defense are like giants."

She stepped back, narrowing her eyes. "Are you okay?"

"Nothing a little TLC from my favorite girl won't cure." I leaned in to kiss her, forgetting we had an audience.

Until my brother made a retching noise.

"Get over here, squirt," I said, crooking my finger. Xander came willingly, wedging himself between Hailee and me.

"We need to talk," she mouthed, flicking her eyes to him.

Dread snaked through me.

Something had happened.

"Are you okay?" I mouthed back, and she nodded, but there was a sadness in her expression that had alarm bells ringing.

But in true Hailee fashion, she pasted on a smile and said, "Right, who wants ice cream?"

"Can I have sprinkles?" Xander slipped out of my arms and stared up at us.

"Of course you can, buddy. You can have whatever you want."

"I want three flavors."

"You got it, Xan."

We moved over to where Mom and Dad were hovering. "Congratulations, Son."

"Thanks, Dad."

"You pulled out a nice play at the end."

"Coach almost blew a gasket."

"I bet. But it paid off."

"Come here, sweetheart." Mom pulled me into a hug. "I'm so proud of you."

She told me every time we were together. It was as if after her illness she wanted to treasure every moment, imprint every memory. She was healthy now, but I guess something like that changed you.

I knew it had changed me to some extent.

"The team not celebrating?" Dad asked as we headed for their SUV.

"Yeah, there'll be a party or something."

"You can always go after we—"

"Don't do that," I said. "I want to be here, with you guys." My arm slipped tighter around Xander.

"You're a good man, Cameron." Dad squeezed my shoulder.

"Thanks." Emotion clogged my throat, but it was nothing compared to the way my heart squeezed at how tight Xander clung to me as we made our way across the parking lot.

21

Hailee

"Is he asleep?" I asked.

"Yeah, finally."

"Come here." Crossing the room to Cameron, I pulled him into my arms. "It's going to be okay."

"Is it?" His voice cracked. "Because I'm not sure anymore."

Xander had wanted to stay with us at the apartment, so we'd agreed he could. Karen and Clarke had watched on with a mix of dejection and relief as we left their car and made our way into the building. They were staying at a hotel two blocks over, but would join us for breakfast in the morning.

"Tell me what he said to you at the game." Cameron stared down at me with so much pain, I wanted to take it from him.

"He asked if we were getting married..." I took a deep breath, knowing how greatly my next words would affect him., "and then he asked if he could move in with us."

"Fuck, he said that?"

I nodded, giving him some space to digest things.

Cameron ran a hand over his head and cupped the back of his neck. "What am I supposed to do here?"

"You just keep doing what you're doing. Xander knows you love him, Cameron. He knows your mom and dad love him. He's just a little messed up right now, but he'll grow out of it."

"Will he?" Cam dropped down onto the edge of the bed, burying his face in his hands. I sat beside him, offering my comfort if he needed it.

"You know, tonight, at the game, I wanted it. I wanted to go pro. I don't know what happened. One minute, I was worrying about Xander and my parents and you, and the next, I was so wrapped up in the game..."

"Hey, don't feel bad." I cupped his face, forcing him to look at me. "You should never feel bad for wanting to follow your dreams, Cam. Ever."

"I still can't believe he said he wants to live with us."

"It's like he's waiting for you to go home."

"I know."

"Do you want that?" I asked, unsure I wanted the answer. "To go back to Rixon?"

"I just want to help him."

"Even if it costs you your dream?"

He let out a weary sigh. "You're looking at me like it's not only my dream I'm sacrificing."

My stomach knotted. "So, you are considering giving everything up?" The words spilled out before I could stop them. "I'm sorry, that's not fair."

It was his brother. His kid brother who had almost lost his mom. I couldn't resent that.

I wouldn't.

Not when I'd pulled him away from them.

"I wish I could wave a magic wand and make all this better for you and Xander."

"I know you do, and I love you for it." Cameron reached for me, fisting the oversized Wolverines t-shirt and pulling me into his arms.

"We get through senior year and then I go home, at least until this stuff with Xander gets better. He needs me, Hailee. I can't just turn my back on him. I can't..." His eyes shuttered, torment etched into the lines of his handsome face. "But if you don't want to follow me, I'll understand. I know you have a better shot at following your dreams here or in Philly."

"Stop." I leaned in touching my head to his. "Where you go, I go."

"Yeah?" Relief washed over him.

"Cameron, as if you need to ask."

"It won't be forever, I promise," he breathed the words as if they were hard to say. "Just until he's in a better place."

"It's okay. He needs you."

"And I need *you*. I will always need you, Hailee. I hope you know that." He stared at me with such intensity, I sucked in a sharp breath.

"I do."

Cameron

"Can't I stay another night?"

"We need to get home, sweetheart," Mom reached for

Xander, but he dodged her advance. The flash of hurt in her eyes gutted me.

"Xander, please, don't make a scene. Cameron and Hailee need to—"

"Hey," I said, finally making myself known. "Are you all set?"

"Yes," my parents said at the same time as Xander grumbled, "No."

"I think Hailee wanted some help, if you two want to—"

"Sure thing." Dad squeezed my shoulder, guiding Mom away.

"Hey, squirt. What's going on?" I sat down beside my brother.

"I don't want to go back to Rixon."

"No? But what about school? Your friends?"

"I know Mom and Dad call you and tell you everything, Cam." He flicked his knowing eyes to mine.

"They're worried. We all are."

"It's not like I try to make people hate me." He shrugged.

"Nobody hates you, Xan." God. He was seven. It was too young to harbor such negativity but here we were.

"Well, they don't like me. Harry Jones and his friends all say I'm weird."

"You are not weird." A sense of protectiveness flooded me, and I wanted nothing more than to call Jase and Asher and ride down to Rixon and hunt down Harry Jones and teach the little punk a lesson or two.

"It's okay, Cam. I know I'm not like most other kids."

Fuck.

His words were so innocent, but there was so much conviction behind them that he might as well have punched his little fist into my chest and ripped out my heart.

"You've gotta tell me how I can fix this, Xander."

He looked at me with big, sad eyes and said, "When are you coming home?"

"As soon as senior year is done, I'll be back. It's not long really, not when you take out the holidays and spring break."

"And then I can come stay with you and Hailee?"

Jesus. This was really happening. My kid brother was choosing me over our parents.

"You can come and stay, yeah. Hailee told me the two of you talked about it?"

"She didn't really give me an answer."

"You'll always be welcome to stay over, Xan, you know that. But Mom and Dad would be really upset if you didn't want to live with them anymore."

"But I want to live with you." He twisted his hands in his lap.

I wanted to ask him why, to make him tell me why he felt this way, but I knew he didn't have the answers. If he did, we wouldn't be sitting here right now.

"Xan, look at me." I slid my fingers under his chin and tilted his face to mine. "Do you have any idea how much we all love you?" His lip quivered. "Mom and Dad would do anything to make you happy, but you need to talk to them, buddy. They can't help if they don't know what's wrong."

Silent tears began rolling down his cheeks and he wrapped his arms around me, burying his face into my chest. "I don't want anyone to leave me, not again," he murmured against my sweater.

"Seven months, Xan," I said, rubbing his back. "Seven months and I'll be home." But as I said the words, I already knew I'd be looking at my schedule to see where I could make more trips back to Rixon. I couldn't ignore this, not anymore. Something was going on with Xander, something huge, and he needed me.

———

"Hey, you don't call, you never write," Asher chuckled. "I'm beginning to think you don't love me anymore."

"I texted you just the other day."

"Text smext. I need to hear your voice."

"I'm hanging up—"

"Relax, I'm just busting your balls. What's up?"

"I need to cancel guys weekend."

"What?" he gasped. "No way!"

We'd arranged a weekend away since we all had the same bye week. It never happened, so we'd planned on making the most of it.

"I'm going home, I need to—"

"Xander?"

"Yeah. He needs me."

"So, we'll all go," he said, as if it was the simplest answer.

"But we have the tickets." We were going to catch an Eagles game. Jase's dad had some old friends in high places and they'd managed to get us VIP passes.

"Xander is more important. We can take him to a Rixon Raiders game and boost his cool-o-meter. The girls will be lining up for a chance with the Xan-man."

"Ash, he's seven." I pinched the bridge of my nose.

"Nothing wrong with starting early."

"I can't believe they gave you your foster license." He and Mya had been approved over the summer. They didn't plan to become active foster parents until after graduation, but they had wanted to be prepared.

"What? The kids love me." He chuckled. "But seriously, me and Jase can come with you. Xander will love it. We'll be like the four amigos causing chaos. Just like old times."

"I appreciate it, Ash, I do, but..."

"You need some bro time?"

"Yeah, I think we do. He's got this crazy idea into his head that he wants to live with me and Hailee when we move back to Rixon."

"Hold up." I heard the surprise in his voice. "You made the decision?"

"Yeah, I think so. He's getting worse. My mom and dad don't know what to do with him anymore. Things will be easier if I'm around."

"I get it, I do, and I hope you don't think I'm talking out of line here, but do you think that's the right move?"

"What do you mean?" My brows bunched together.

"Xander is already incredibly attached to you. If you go back, it might only compound that. He needs to deal with whatever it is going on in his head. The counselor should be able to help."

Xander had recently started sessions with a new therapist. But he was resistant, unable to articulate why he felt the way he felt.

"How are your mom and dad holding up?"

"It's taking its toll. Mom isn't sleeping and my dad just throws himself into work and then feels guilty."

"That's rough. I'm sorry, Cam. If there's anything we can do..."

"Thank you. I'm hoping if I'm around more, he'll settle down at school. I made him a calendar of every weekend I'll be home."

It had been Hailee's idea. We'd printed it out and it doubled as a countdown until graduation. Mom had helped Xander pin it on his wall beside his bed, and every morning, he crossed off another day.

I couldn't get back to Rixon every weekend, not with games, but I'd managed to work it so I could go home at least once a month. Then there were longer holidays like Thanksgiving and Christmas.

It was a lot to juggle but I needed to make it work.

"So if you're planning on returning to Rixon after graduation," his voice sobered, "what does that mean for the draft?"

"I haven't gotten that far yet."

Xander needed me *now*. He needed to know I planned

on being around more. Everything else had to take a backseat for now.

"I get it. I'm here, whatever you or your family needs."

We chatted for a little bit longer. I asked about Mya and we talked about Hailee's latest installation at an independent gallery in the city. By the time we hung up, I felt lighter.

Talking to my best friends had that effect on me. We'd been through so much together. It felt good knowing that they always had my back, no matter what.

Over three years apart, but we were stronger than ever.

Brothers bound by choice not blood.

Family.

And I wouldn't change them for the world.

22

Hailee

Senior year wasn't quite what I expected. I thought Cameron and I would enjoy our last year of college, that I would flourish with my art and he would carve out a name for himself among NFL scouts.

The reality was quite a bit different.

After that first game, when his parents and Xander had visited, Cameron began splitting his time between Michigan and Rixon as much as he could.

Sometimes I went with him, but most of the time, I didn't. I had classes, friends, various installations across the city.

I had a life... *here*.

But more and more, his life became back in Rixon.

I watched him pack his weekend bag with a tightness across my chest. It was the third time this month.

"I thought you were going to try to stick to the schedule," I said.

"I was." He leaned down and kissed my hair. "But Xander has been doing better. I don't want to ruin all his progress."

"But what about classes Monday?"

"I spoke to Professor Joffrey. As long as I get a copy of the notes and submit my essay on time, he's happy to excuse me."

"And practice?" The team were on a winning streak, and Coach Byford was determined for them to go all the way to playoffs.

"I'll be back. I told Xan it's a fly-by visit. If I leave tonight—"

"Tonight?"

"Yeah, I thought I told you that was the plan?" Cam stuffed another t-shirt in his bag.

"We just got home, it's late." Not to mention the fact he'd just played a football game. "You can leave in the morning. You'll be there tomorrow night and then you can have all day Sunday together."

"I promised him I'd take him to the park."

"You can't go to the park Sunday?"

"Hailee..." Cam paused what he was doing and lifted his eyes to mine. "I need to do this."

"I know. I just don't like the idea of you driving through the night after a game."

"I'll be careful, I promise. I'll stop halfway and get some rest."

My lips pursed. I didn't like the sound of that any better.

"What?" he asked.

"I just worry you're pushing yourself too hard. I know you want to help Xander, but you can't be everything to everyone, Cam. Something has to give eventually."

And the way we were headed, I was starting to wonder if it was me.

If I was the thing to give.

Between practice, classes, and going back and forth to Rixon, Cameron was barely here anymore. Yet, I couldn't say anything, because if I did, it made me a terrible person.

So I stuffed down my reservations, put on a smile, and played my role as supportive, understanding girlfriend.

And it was slowly breaking my heart.

"It isn't forever. The holidays will be here soon enough, and then once it's the new year, and he knows there are only a few months before graduation, I think it'll be easier."

Cameron was in too deep to see that he was feeding Xander's attachment issues. I knew Asher had tried to talk to him about it; Mya had told me the last time we spoke. But again, I didn't feel able to say anything because Xander was his brother. His baby brother. And after what they went through almost losing their mom... I couldn't criticize his choices.

Even if I didn't fully understand them.

"I think I'm done." He zipped the bag and stood, running a hand through his damp hair. "I'll see you Monday, okay?"

I nodded, a rush of emotion clawing up my throat.

"Please be safe, and call me when you stop, no matter the time."

"I'll text. You need to get some sleep."

Like that would come easy knowing Cameron was on the road in the middle of the night, running on nothing but adrenaline and energy drinks.

"I will." He slid his hand along my jaw and tipped my head back, grazing his lips over mine. "I love you, Hailee."

"I love you too."

I went to deepen the kiss, but Cameron had already pulled away, slinging his bag over his shoulder and making for the door.

While I stood there watching as he took another piece of my heart with him.

———

I woke to the sound of my cell phone blaring. A smile tugged at my lips at the prospect of speaking to Cameron, but when I saw Felicity's name, disappointment snaked through me.

"Hey," I said, around a yawn.

"Did I wake you?"

"I must have fallen asleep."

"Late night?"

"I barely slept. Cameron drove back to Rixon through the night and I couldn't settle."

"I thought he was going this morning?"

"Me too," I said, my chest tightening.

"He's going home a lot, huh?"

"Yeah, I guess..." I trailed off, unsure of what she wanted me to say.

Everyone knew Cameron was going back and forth. It wasn't some big secret. But it did make me wonder what our friends were saying about it.

"Has Jason said anything?"

"Like what?" Felicity asked.

"I don't know... ignore me."

"Hailee, did something happen?"

"No... yes..." I released a weary sigh. "I don't know."

"Okay," she said, "start from the beginning."

So I did. I told her how Cameron and I made the calendar for Xander, how it was supposed to help him count off the days until he saw his brother. I told her how the visits were becoming more and more regular, and the time we spent together was becoming less and less. I even told her how we'd barely been intimate lately.

"What, like no sex, *at all*?"

"We've fooled around a little, but no, no sex."

"God, Hails, how are you functioning right now? I can't go more than a couple of days."

"It's not by choice, trust me."

Cameron was always too tired or too wound up to get into it, so I'd stopped trying.

"I feel like we're drifting apart, and I don't know what to do about it. And I hate myself for even thinking it because it's Xander. Of course Cameron should be there for him."

"Well, yeah. But you're important too, babe. He shouldn't be neglecting your relationship either."

"How do I say anything without coming across as a selfish, horrible person though?"

"I'm thinking it's less about saying anything and more about finding the spark again."

"The spark?" I said with skepticism.

"Yeah, you know, put on something sexy and wait for him to come home and then seduce him."

I smothered a groan. "Sometimes I really wish you wouldn't suggest things you clearly do with my step-brother."

"It's just sex, babe. Everyone does it."

Some more than others apparently.

"Do you think I'm crazy?" Because I was starting to feel that way.

"What? *No!* No way. You're totally justified to feel upset."

"I'm not upset, Fee, I'm just..." Oh, who I was trying to kid? I *was* upset and that only made me feel guiltier which in turn upset me more.

I was a mess.

All because my boyfriend was trying to do right by his family.

"It's okay. You're entitled to your feelings, just don't let them fester. Cameron loves you Hailee, so much. Besides, if he ever hurt you, Jase would—"

"Don't you dare tell him any of this." Panic welled inside of me.

"I won't."

"I mean it, Felicity. It's bad enough I have to listen to your freaky sex talk knowing you're boning my brother, without you discussing my sex life with him."

"But he could talk to Cam and—"

"Felicity, I'm serious. I will revoke your best friend status if you breathe even so much as a word of this to Jason."

"Relax, I'm joking."

"You'd better be." Because I was not ready to get relationship advice from Jason, no matter how close we were these days. "I'm sure things will be okay. It's just a weird time."

"Atta girl. And don't forget what I said about seducing him. You can thank me later," she added, and I rolled my eyes.

"Yep. Got it," I said, wanting to end this line of conversation.

"Let me know how it goes."

"Hm-hmm, talk to you soon. Bye."

"Hailee, wait—"

I hung up, letting out an exasperated breath. A second later, my cell pinged.

Flick: Rude much? It's a good thing I love you. Call me soon xo

I chuckled. I couldn't help it. Since Jason had proposed almost two years ago, Felicity had morphed into this confident, sexy, no-holds-barred kind of woman. I didn't blame her. She was engaged to one of the NCAA's players of the decade. Jason had already earned himself numerous records, and a spot in the Hall of Fame. And ESPN were already naming him as a sure thing for next year's draft. It wasn't just Jason though, it was her. After a rocky start, Flick had found her feet with her studies. She had everything going for her. The guy, the career... the huge diamond ring on her finger.

I'd been nothing but happy for them when Jason proposed. Same with Asher and Mya. But another year had gone by, and Cameron still hadn't popped the question. I wasn't in a rush, I wasn't. But lately, I couldn't help but wonder if he was just waiting for the right time... or if he was stalling.

"Ugh, stop," I hissed at myself.

I was letting my mind play tricks on me. Just because Cameron wanted to be there for Xander, it wasn't any reflection on our relationship.

So why couldn't I seem to separate the two?

And why, every time he left, did it feel like the space between us grew?

Cameron

"Hailee, I'm home." I threw my keys down and kicked off my sneakers. I was bone-tired and weary. It had been a long ride back to Michigan, only made ten times worse given how badly Xander had reacted when it was time for me to leave. It had taken almost two hours to calm him, and then I'd wanted to stick around and make sure he was okay, which meant I'd missed practice.

It was late, past ten.

The lingering smell of lasagna wafted down the hall. But it wasn't until I entered the kitchen and saw the barely touched meal, I knew I'd fucked up twice today.

Our small table was set for two, complete with candles

and wine glasses, and a glass of freshly cut flowers. Trudging to the refrigerator, I was hardly surprised to find a bottle of wine chilling and a container of our favorite dessert from the restaurant across the street. Hailee had gone to a lot of trouble, yet, she'd never said a word.

Because she wanted to surprise you, asshole.

I let out a frustrated groan. I hadn't texted. After sending the initial text to say I was leaving, I'd been so caught up with Xander and then my own thoughts, I'd completely forgotten to text her.

Pulling my lifeless cell phone out of my pocket, I plugged it into a power outlet and waited for it to come to life.

I had text after text from Hailee.

Hailee: It's me. You said you'd be home by now but you're not here and your cell is ringing out. Let me know you're okay.

Hailee: Since you're still not answering, I called your mom. She said you left Rixon at one. What the hell, Cameron? You texted me at eight this morning and said you were leaving. What is going on?

. . .

Hailee: I consider myself a pretty understanding person... but what the actual fuck, Cameron? It's almost nine-thirty and I'm going to bed. Not that I imagine I'll get any sleep because my boyfriend is unreachable, and no one has spoken to him all day.

Guilt trickled down my spine. It seemed so fucking inexcusable now, but at the time, after leaving Xander, all I'd wanted was some time with my thoughts. One hour had turned into two and two into four. I'd made one quick stop for gas and to use the restroom and then got back on the road.

I hadn't stopped to think about Hailee.

I hadn't stopped to think about anything besides my kid brother back home, breaking his heart because I was leaving him again.

It was *all* I could think about.

And, in this moment, I realized how screwed up that was. I'd taken a lot for granted these last few weeks. Hailee. The team. My classes.

Hailee.

Fuck.

I glanced at the table again. She'd planned an entire romantic evening and I hadn't even fucking called her to tell her the change of plans.

With a heavy heart, I moved through the apartment to our bedroom. It was quiet, but nothing could have prepared me for the sight of Hailee asleep on the top of the bed, clutching a pillow, her new lingerie accentuating her womanly curves.

She hadn't just planned a romantic meal; she'd planned a night of seduction. Probably in hopes of rekindling our usually healthy sex life. But with everything lately, I was normally too exhausted.

In fact, I couldn't remember the last time we were intimate. I wracked my brain. There had been the night a few weeks back, against the wall. Surely it hadn't been that long?

Crap.

I'd royally fucked up.

"Way to go, Chase" I grumbled to myself. She'd fallen asleep crying, that much was obvious, and it cracked my heart wide open.

"I'm sorry." I moved nearer, brushing the hairs from her eyes. Hailee stirred but didn't wake, so I wiggled the covers free from underneath her body and pulled them up over her.

"I'll make this up to you, I promise," I whispered.

Because I would.

One way or another, I would find a way to show Hailee how much I loved her.

23

Cameron

When I woke up, Hailee was gone. The bedsheets were cold and the hole she left was vast.

I ran a hand down my face before leaning over and grabbing my cell phone off the nightstand.

Me: I'm sorry.

I waited.

And waited.

But nothing came.

I didn't blame her. Roles reversed, I'd be pissed too.

My fingers flew over the screen.

Me: I'll make it up to you, I promise.

My cell pinged, but it wasn't the name I wanted to see.

· · ·

Jase: What the fuck did you do to my sister?

Jesus. She'd told him? Okay, I knew the likelihood was that Hailee had told Felicity and she'd told Jase, but still, I didn't like thinking they all knew what a selfish asshole I'd been.

It had been a lapse in judgment. I'd taken for granted that Hailee would be waiting, that she'd understand where I was coming from.

A whole day, asshole. I ignored the little voice of reason and climbed out of bed. I needed a shower and some food since I'd gone to bed on an empty stomach.

Hitting call, I waited for Jase to answer.

"I fucked up."

"Yeah, you did," he ground out. "What the hell were you thinking? She was going out of her damn mind."

"I didn't... shit, Jase. Things were hard with Xan when I went to leave. He was a mess, I was a mess. I just needed space, ya know?"

"I get it. He's going through some stuff and you're carrying that responsibility, but Hailee is your—"

Everything.

She was my everything.

"Yeah, I know," I forced the words out over the lump in my throat.

"Talk to me, Cam. Where's your head at?"

"He needs me, that's all I know. When I'm there, he's better, and Mom and Dad can breathe again."

"Shit, it's that bad?"

"Yeah. His therapist is talking about attachment disorder. But his symptoms are atypical. Kids with AD don't usually form secure attachments to any of their caregivers, but he's become overly attached to me." I inhaled a shaky breath.

Xander was seven. Every year that passed since my mom's illness, he'd withdrawn more and more. It was as if he wanted to escape my parents when they offered him nothing but love and comfort.

I hated it.

I hated that I didn't understand why he felt that way, even though I knew it wasn't something he chose to feel.

The whole situation made me feel powerless, but being there for him, for my parents, was something I *could* do. It was something I could control.

"He'll get through this, Cam," Jase said. "You all will."

"It's just something I have to do."

"I get it. So does Hailee. Just don't shut her out, okay? You need her."

"I know." Pain laced my words. "I'll fix it."

"Good, because I really don't want to have to drive up to Michigan and kick your ass." I heard the smirk in his words.

"You think you could take me?"

"I know I could."

"You wish, asshole." Laughter rumbled in my chest and it felt good.

I couldn't remember the last time I laughed.

"How's stuff with the team?" he asked.

"Coach is going to tear me a new one for missing practice."

"He'll understand."

"You haven't met Coach Byford." I hesitated, hardly able to believe the words teetering on the tip of my tongue.

"What?" Jason asked.

"Nothing." I couldn't say it. Not to him.

"Shit, Cam," he breathed. "Tell me you're not seriously considering quitting the team? In your *senior year*?"

"I don't want to." I didn't. "But it means I could go home at the weekend and travel back for classes."

"And what is my sister supposed to do while you're driving back and forth?"

"Jase, come on..."

"I'm not trying to be a dick, I'm not. But we literally just spent five minutes going over the fact you need to let Hailee in, not push her away."

"It's not like that. I just..."

Jase let out an exasperated breath. "You need to figure out your priorities here, Cam. Graduation is in less than seven months. Less than six if you take out the holidays and spring break. It isn't that long. If you walk from the team, you'll regret it."

"But if I don't, and Xander gets worse..." How could I live with that?

"I wish I had the answer," he sighed.

"Yeah, me too."

"Just talk to Hailee. Any decisions you do or don't make need to be done with her. It's only fair."

"I will, I promise." If she wanted to talk to me anytime soon that was.

"I gotta shoot, Felicity is—"

"Yeah, yeah. Go tend to your girl." I smiled. Jase was different but he wore it well.

"I'm here, Cam. Always."

We said goodbye and I hung up. Opening my message history with Hailee, I started typing.

Me: We need to talk.

Hailee

I stared at Cameron's message, the permanent knot in my stomach tightening.

He wanted to talk.

My mind automatically assumed he wanted to talk about us... and I hated it.

I hated that I was that girl now, insecure and uncertain of her relationship, of her man. But last night, after the gnawing worry, followed by frustration and then a deep sense of disappointment, I'd fallen to sleep clutching my tear-stained pillow.

The vibration of my cell jerked me from my reverie.

Cameron: Hailee, please.

. . .

Hailee: Okay.

Cameron: I have practice straight after classes but after? At the apartment?

Hailee: I'll be there.

Pocketing my phone, I made my way toward the Art and Architecture building for my morning classes. I didn't know how things had gotten to this point, but I didn't know how to fix them either.

"Hailee," Devyn waved as she approached me. "I'm glad I caught up to you."

I frowned.

"Dominic said Cameron missed practice. Something about an emergency at home? I hope everything's okay?"

Devyn was a sweetheart. She was Dominic's twin sister and the two of them were best friends. So much so, they shared an apartment off-campus. She also happened to be a huge football fan, so Cameron and I hung out with them a lot during the season.

"It's Xander, he's going through some stuff."

"That must be rough, the age gap." She hooked her arm through mine as we headed into the building. "Cameron is a good brother."

"He is." I really didn't want to talk about this.

"You know, I heard my brother and a couple of the guys talking... Crap, this is going to sound so wrong..."

"Just spit it out, Dev," I said, smothering my irritation.

"They're worried." She gave me a sympathetic smile. "He never hangs out with them anymore; he's distracted at practice... they're saying his heart's not in it anymore. There's even talk of Coach giving the second string more time on the field."

Her words reverberated through me, but Devyn wasn't done. "Has he said anything to you? Doesn't he want to play any—"

"What? *No*! Cameron loves the team. He'd never walk out on them. He's just finding it hard to balance everything."

"That's what I told Dominic. Cam knows there's too much on the line this season. Especially since the championship should have been theirs last year." She let out a little huff.

"Listen, Dev, it was good to see you," I rushed out, "but I need to use the bathroom before class. Catch you later?"

"Huh, sure." Her lips curved. "I'm sorry if I overstepped—"

"You didn't. I just really need to pee." Offering her a small wave, I hurried down the hall toward the nearest bathroom. Inside, I ducked into the first stall and closed the door, inhaling a ragged breath.

The guys thought Cameron wanted to quit.

I knew things had been tough, but I didn't realize it was affecting his performance so much.

Because he didn't tell you.

My heart sank.

When Cameron's mom had gotten sick, he'd turned to me. I had been his person. His safe place. But he wasn't turning to me now.

Whether he realized it or not, Cam was shutting me out.

And I was letting him.

Cameron

Blood roared between my ears as I sat and waited for Hailee to get home. We hadn't spoken again all day, despite me reaching for my cell at least five times.

There was so much I wanted to say to her, to explain, but every time I tried to start typing, I couldn't find the words.

I hoped talking face to face would go better.

The door opened and I heard the soft thud of her sneakers against the floor. "I'm in here," I called, and seconds later, Hailee appeared.

"Hey." She gave me a tentative smile.

I wanted to go to her, to pull her into my arms and beg for forgiveness, but there were things we needed to discuss. Things I needed to say without the distraction of her close proximity.

"Sit, please."

She did, folding her hands into her lap.

"I owe you an apology. I fucked up, and I'm sorry. I'm so fucking sorry."

"I just don't understand..." she said. "I know things are

hard right now, but you didn't even think to call me. Do you have any idea what that feels like?"

"I... I'm sorry."

"Wait." She held up her hand, silencing me. "I'm going to ask you something and I want the truth, Cam. I think I deserve it."

"Okay..." My brows furrowed, not liking the finality in her tone.

"Do you want to quit the team?"

I reared back, my eyes growing to saucers. "How did you—"

I was going to kill Jason.

"So it's true?" Disappointment washed over her, the distance between us vaster than ever.

"No... I mean, I thought about it, but—"

"You thought it about it and you never said a word. What is happening to us, Cameron? Because when the semester started and you began pulling away, I told myself it was just the pressure of balancing everything. Then you started going back and forth to Rixon more and more, and I got it, because it's Xander. He's your blood, your family. But what I didn't anticipate was that every time you left, it would drive the wedge growing between us deeper.

"I think I've been understanding. I've tried to be there for you, for Xander, even your parents. I don't grumble or complain, or trash talk you to our friends. Because I get it. I get you want to do the right thing. You wouldn't be the guy I fell in love with if you didn't. But something is happening to us and I'm starting to wonder if it has anything to do with everything else going on, or if it's just us. If maybe you're starting to feel like..." Hailee's bottom lip quivered but she swallowed her emotion. "*I'm* the burden."

Without speaking, I got up and crossed the room to her. Dropping to my knees, I looped my hand around the back of her neck and pulled her to me until our heads were pressed together. "You are not a burden."

"So, what is it? Why do I feel like I'm losing you?"

Her words snaked through me, lashing my insides. "Because I'm an asshole," I breathed. "I take your love for granted. I take *you* for granted, and I shouldn't."

"I just don't understand how we got here?" Hailee was holding back her tears. I heard them in her voice.

"I love you. I love you so damn much, and I know things haven't been right for a while and I—"

The blare of my cell cut through the air, and Hailee's gaze darted over my shoulder.

"I'll leave it," I said.

But it didn't stop ringing.

"Maybe you should get it; it could be your mom."

My eyes shuttered, my heart torn in two. I wanted to put Hailee first, to prove to her she was the most important thing in my life...

"Cam, it's okay." She took my hands and gently moved out of my hold. "Go, they need you."

And I need you. But the words wouldn't come out.

I got up and ran a hand over my face. Hailee had curled up on the chair, her expression crestfallen. "I'm sorry," I mouthed as I snatched up my cell phone and hit answer. "Dad?" I said, panic flooding me as I wondered what Xander could have possibly done this time.

"Cameron, Son..."

"Dad, what is it?"

"It's your mom... She's in the hospital."

The world fell away as I tried to process his words.

"What do you mean, she's in the hospital?"

"She... she collapsed. They think she had a seizure."

"Where's Xander?"

"He's with Asher's mom. He was there when it happened. I found them—"

"Dad?" My voice cracked.

"We need you, Son. We need you to come home."

24

Hailee

We got a flight to Philadelphia and rented a car to drive to Rixon. It was the quickest option.

Cameron had barely spoken a word on the ninety-minute flight from Detroit. He'd clutched my hand the entire way there though, as if I was his lifeline.

The second I pulled up outside the Rixon General, Cameron grabbed the door handle. "I need to—"

"Go," I said. "I'll find somewhere to park."

He gave me a small nod and climbed out, jogging across the street and disappearing inside.

My heart ached for them. First Xander, now this. I didn't want to assume the worst, but I knew that if anything happened to Karen, the Chase men wouldn't survive it.

I found a parking spot and cut the engine. I wanted to go to him, to see how Karen was. But I needed a minute.

I didn't get it though. My cell phone started ringing.

"Jason?"

"How is he?"

"I- I don't know. His dad called and everything was a blur after that. We just got to the hospital."

"Is he there? Can I speak to him? He isn't answering his cell."

"N- no. I'm in the car still."

"Hailee, what is it? What's wrong?"

The tears I'd fought so hard to contain exploded, streaming down my cheeks like unstoppable rivers, the noise of my heavy sobs audible.

"Shit, Hailee, don't cry. He'll be okay. They'll all be okay."

"They won't. If she doesn't make it... I'll lose him, Jase. I know I will." Every fear and insecurity I'd felt over the last few weeks battered me like an unforgiving storm.

If his mom was sick again, he would quit the team—maybe even quit college—and move back to Rixon. Because that's the kind of guy Cameron was. He made sacrifices for the people he loved. And they would need him.

His family would need him.

"You're his family too," Jase said, and I didn't even realize I'd said the words aloud.

"You know what I mean. He'll be here and I'll be there."

"But you'll get through this. You will. Listen, did the two of you get a chance to talk?"

"We were talking when his dad called. Why?"

"Cameron loves you, Hailee. He needs you. I know it might not always seem like that, but we're guys, we get shit wrong sometimes. Don't give up on him, okay?"

Silence filled the line. I wanted to heed his words, to be a pillar of strength for Cameron and his family, but the truth was, I was scared... scared of what the future would bring for us.

"It was you, you know?" Jason's voice grounded me.

"What was?"

"It was you and Cam that made me realize there's more to life than football."

I snorted. "You hated me back then."

"I didn't hate you, Hailee. I just..."

"Yeah, I know."

We had a lot of history—a lot of bad history—but we weren't those people anymore. Jason was one of the most important people in my life.

He was family.

"Cameron loves you and even if he tries to push you away or cut you loose, it'll only be because he thinks he's doing right by you. If his mom is sick again, and I really fucking hope she isn't," he let out a weary sigh, "you're going to need to be his strength, Sis. Even when he doesn't think he wants you to be."

More tears flowed down my cheeks and I bit back a huge sob.

"You hear me?" Jase said. "You might not be a Ford, Hailee, but you are my sister in all the ways that matter. And we don't quit, okay? We fight."

"Yeah, okay."

"Good, now go be with our guy. And tell him I'm here. Whatever he needs, all he has to do is call."

"Thank you, Jason."

"Anytime. Now brush yourself off and be the badass Hailee Raine I know you can be."

Cameron

"Dad."

His head snapped up and he was out of his chair in a second, rushing toward me and pulling me into his arms. "You're here, thank God, you're here."

"How is she? What are they saying?"

"They're still running tests."

"Do they think it's the same as before?"

He paled. "It's the most likely scenario, Son."

Fuck.

"But they said she was okay. She got the all clear." Mom had the surgery and they'd gotten the tumor.

"We always knew this was a possibility, Cameron."

Yeah, but how unlucky did someone have to be to have it come back? I couldn't get my head around that. Hadn't we dealt with enough already?

"Xander—"

"He's okay." Dad squeezed my shoulder. "I checked in with Julia earlier."

But I knew the truth. Xander wasn't okay.

"It's like he knew," I said.

"Whatever do you mean?"

"It's like he knew she was going to get sick again and that's why he kept pushing her away."

"Cameron, he didn't know. He couldn't have."

Of course, I knew that. But it didn't stop me wondering if he sensed something.

"Hailee," Dad's gaze moved over my shoulder.

"Hi, Clarke. I'm so sorry." She didn't think twice about hugging him.

"I'm glad you're here." Dad held her at arm's length, offering her a warm smile.

"I wouldn't be anywhere else."

My chest squeezed, remembering the conversation we'd been having as my dad called. The conversation we still needed to have.

The conversation that would have to take a backseat.

"Shall I get us some coffee?" Hailee suggested. It was late, but I wasn't leaving until I got to see Mom.

"That's a great idea," Dad said, digging out his wallet. "Here, let me—"

"Don't worry, I've got it." She offered him a smile.

"Thank you," I said, and Hailee took off down the hall.

"I'm so glad she came with you, Son. You're lucky to have her."

He was right, I was.

Hailee hadn't given coming with me a second thought. She'd gotten on her phone the second I told her I needed to get to Rixon ASAP.

But I couldn't stop thinking about what she'd said earlier.

I couldn't stop wondering if she was right.

———

It was almost eleven when they finally let us in to see Mom. The doctor confirmed that she'd had a seizure due to a new glioma.

My mom had *another* brain tumor.

I didn't know what the fuck to do with that.

"I'll give the three of you some space," Hailee said as we reached Mom's room.

"Thank you." Dad slipped inside, but I stayed back.

"I'm not sure I can do this again," I confessed, my heart numb from the news.

"Sure, you can." Hailee enveloped me in her slim arms. "You're so strong, Cam. And I'm here, I'm right here. Whatever you need."

I wanted to tell her to take me away from here. To hold me tight and never let go. But my dad needed me, my mom too. And Xander.

Fuck... Xander.

"This will destroy Xander." I swallowed hard, dropping my gaze to the floor.

"Look at me," Hailee said, sliding her hand to my cheek. "You can do this, Cameron. They need you."

Touching my head to hers, I tried to draw comfort from her. The girl who had stood up beside me through this once already.

"I can't lose her, Hailee. I just can't."

"Ssh," she whispered. "We don't know the prognosis yet. Go be with her and your dad. We'll worry about the rest later." Hailee's lips hovered over mine, touching but not kissing. I felt her uncertainty, and I knew I'd been the one to put it there.

But I couldn't do this, not right now. Not when I didn't know if my mom was going to make it or not.

"I won't be long," I said, pulling away.

"Okay, I'll be right out here." Hailee stepped back, wrapping her arms around her chest, barely able to meet my gaze.

I should have apologized, explained that my head was all over the place. But I didn't.

I couldn't.

Because this wasn't like before.

This time, I couldn't afford to fall apart. Not when my family were already holding on by a thread. This time, I had to step up to the plate and be the brother Xander needed, the son my parents needed.

This time, I had to put them first.

Hailee

"Hi, sweetheart." My mom came to me in a dream, only when I opened my eyes, she was standing right there.

"Mom?" I pushed up, my muscles sore from sleeping on the row of plastic hospital chairs. "What time is it?"

"A little after one."

It had been two hours since Cameron and his dad had disappeared into Karen's room.

"I must have fallen asleep."

She nodded. "Cameron called and asked me to come and get you."

"He did?" I frowned, glancing down the hall where I knew he was with his parents.

"They're going to stay with Karen. He didn't want you to be out here all by yourself."

"Oh, okay." My stomach dipped.

"Come on, sweetheart. Let's go home."

But as I got up and let her lead me away, all I could think was I was leaving my home behind in that room.

"It's so good to see you, Hailee. I just wish it was under better circumstances." Mom made small talk as we walked to her car. It was dark out, a blanket of stars kissing the inky sky. Such a beautiful scene for such a tragic night.

"Did Cameron say anything else?"

"Just that he didn't want you to be alone and that you needed to get some rest too."

I toyed with my cell phone, desperate to text him. But I knew he needed some time with his mom and dad to come to terms with everything.

"It's such a shame. Karen is a good woman."

"She is."

We climbed into the car and I let my head fall against the glass, fighting the wave of tears building inside me.

"Hailee?" Mom asked. "Are you okay?"

"I'm fine," I murmured.

And then I puked all over myself.

———

I was sick.

By the time Mom had gotten me home, I could barely stand. At first, I'd thought it was just an emotional response to everything that had happened, but I spent most of the night with my head down the toilet bowl.

"How are you feeling?" Mom slipped into my room with a glass of ice-cold water and some crackers.

"Like I got hit by a truck." I tried to sit up but my stomach roiled.

"Have you heard from Cameron?"

"Nothing." I stared at my cell, willing it to vibrate.

"I'm sure he'll call. It's a lot for them to process." She placed the glass down and pressed her hand against my forehead. "You don't feel feverish. It could be something you ate, or a stomach flu."

"I'll be okay." I brushed her off.

"Cameron will probably have to stay away if he's going to be visiting his mom in the hospital. At least until it passes."

Great.

Just what I didn't need.

"I'm really tired, Mom." I'd barely slept a wink.

"Sure, baby. I'll let you get some rest. If you need anything..."

"I know, and thanks, for everything."

"Hailee, you're my daughter. I will always be here for you. I hope you know that." She gave me a warm smile, before leaving me alone.

The door had barely closed before the first tear fell.

25

Hailee

After twenty-four hours, I finally felt human again. But my heart was still bruised. Cameron had texted a couple of times to say he was spending the day with Xander, and that he would stop by later today.

That was five hours ago.

Mom insisted, I rest. She also insisted I drink regular fluids and nibble crackers to replenish myself. I think secretly she just loved having someone in the house to fuss over.

"Can I get you anything else?" she called, and I shook my head with silent laughter.

"I'm good, Mom, thanks."

"Okay, baby. Holler if you need me."

Our relationship hadn't always been easy, but she was trying. And after Karen's devastating news, I knew I probably needed to try harder.

I wanted to call Cameron, to see how his mom was doing, and to ask if they knew anything more. But I didn't want to crowd him.

So, I opted for calling my best friend instead.

"Hailee, thank God," Felicity said on the third ring.

"I've been so worried. How are you? And Cam? And Karen. Oh God, Karen..."

"Breathe, Flick," I chuckled softly, not that anything about this situation was funny.

"Seriously, how are you?"

"I feel a bit better now, but it wasn't pretty."

"I can't believe you got so sick. Do you think it was something you ate?"

"I don't know. But I feel okay now."

"Well, that's good. And Cam? He must be beside himself."

"I don't really know. He's with Xander."

"You mean you haven't seen him today?" She sounded surprised.

"Well, no. My mom thought he should stay away until I knew it was only a twenty-four-hour thing."

"Makes sense, I guess. But you've spoken to him, right?"

"I..."

"Hailee?"

"He needs to be with his family right now," I said, unable to keep the sadness out of my voice.

"But you're his family."

I'd thought so too, once upon a time. But I wasn't so sure about anything anymore.

"Has Jason spoken to him?"

"Yeah, they talked earlier."

I sucked in a harsh breath.

"Shit, Hails, I didn't mean to—"

"It's okay. I'm glad he has Jason to talk to."

If he wasn't going to turn to me, he needed to turn to someone.

"I just don't understand it. You've always been so good together."

Her words made the knot in my stomach tighten. "He doesn't want to choose," I said quietly.

"But there doesn't have to be a choice, does there?"

There did though. Or at least, I knew Cameron enough to know that's what he thought. He was an all or nothing guy. I'd seen how much it had affected him not being able to be there for Xander. He'd persisted for me. He'd continued our life in Michigan... *for me*.

But I realized now, his heart wasn't in it.

"He needs to be here with his family."

"You really think he'll quit the team? Leave college?"

I didn't want to believe it when we'd first talked about it, but Karen's diagnosis changed everything. And I knew... in my heart of hearts, I knew I'd already lost him.

Silent tears clung to my lashes.

"I'm so sorry," Felicity said as if she'd worked it out too.

"It's okay," I choked out. "He needs to be here for them."

Even though I knew the words to be true, it didn't make them hurt any less.

"Hailee," Mom yelled. "Cameron is here. I'm going to meet Kent for dinner. We'll be back later."

"Listen, I've got to go."

"Do you want me to come there? I can drive down—"

"No," I said, drying my eyes. "I'll be okay."

"Well, call me later."

"I will. Bye." I hung up and took a deep breath.

"Hailee?" Cameron's voice made my heart soar, but it quickly crashed back down to Earth.

"Come in."

The second he stepped into the room, I saw my greatest fear etched into every single line of his face.

He looked at me with sad eyes and said, "I think we need to talk."

Cameron

"It's okay," Hailee said, completely catching me off guard. I'd come here prepared for a battle. After spending the day with Xander trying to figure out how to tell the girl I loved more than anything that I couldn't be the guy she needed right now, I still didn't know how to say the words.

To tell her I needed to be there for my family.

Yet, she was sitting there, with nothing but resignation in her sad expression.

"You don't need to do this, Cameron. I know what you came here to say, and it's okay."

I blinked, hardly able to believe my ears. "I— I don't understand. What exactly are you saying?"

"I would never ask you to choose between me and them. You need to be here, more than ever. I get it, and it's okay."

Relief slammed into me. She got it.

Fuck, she got it.

"Thank you." I went and sat beside her on the edge of the bed. "I need to do this, for Xander, for them." My voice shook as I tried to find the words. "She's terminal, Hailee. They can make her comfortable and give her meds to manage the symptoms, but there is no surgery this time or magic fix."

"Oh my god, Cameron." She threw her arms around me and I sank into her embrace. It had been the hardest thirty-six hours of my life. I'd spent all day with Xander trying to explain everything to him and then picking up the pieces of his meltdown as his developing brain tried to process things.

"I'm so sorry." Her tears splashed on my sweater.

I cupped Hailee's face, touching my head to hers. "Your mom said you were sick?"

"I'm okay now."

Our lips were so close I could almost taste her, but I didn't come here for this. I came to tell her I needed time and space to be with my family. But now I was here and she was clutching onto me as if I might disappear at any moment, I was overcome with the need to love her. To just *be* with her.

"Cameron?" Her eyes glittered with so much love it gutted me, and I knew if I asked it of her, she would give me whatever I needed.

"Come here." I tried to hold her tighter. I didn't want to be *that* guy, the guy who used sex as a goodbye, but I wanted it.

God, I wanted her.

Hailee made the decision though, sliding her mouth over mine.

"Hailee, wait..." I grabbed her shoulders, swallowing

the ball of emotion lodged in my throat. "I'm not sure this is a good idea."

"I need this," she said, her hands trailing down my chest and tugging my sweater away from my body. "And I know you do too."

"You're sure?"

I was going straight to hell.

I was pretty sure Jason would drag me there anyway after I did this.

But I couldn't stop. Hailee was everything I'd ever wanted. She was strong and good and so fucking selfless, it was breathtaking.

She hadn't made me choose.

She'd given me a gift—she'd let me go.

Hailee climbed onto my lap, kissing me. Small uncertain kisses as my hands slid into her hair, so I could deepen the angle. She traced my lips with her fingers, her tongue. Teasing and tasting. Until the kiss took on a life of its own. Fierce and brutal, as we both fought our demons.

"Is this okay?" I murmured against her lips, as my hands began exploring her body, running them up and down her waist, tracing her soft curves.

She nodded, clawing at my sweater, until I pulled it off my body. Hailee painted letters of love over my skin, branding me with her touch. She felt good, too fucking good.

And you're going to give her up.

I forced down the thoughts. I only wanted to focus on this. Here. Now. On the way Hailee felt so perfect, the way her body fit against mine as if it was made for me, and me alone.

Her clothes went next, her jeans and t-shirt, her black cotton panties. Then my jeans and boxers. Until we were nothing but skin on skin, regrets and apologies.

"I love you, Cameron, so much," she whispered before kissing me deeply.

My dick ached for her, but I didn't want to rush this. I wanted to savor her, imprint this moment to my memory for when things got too tough and I needed to distract myself from the gaping hole in my chest.

I buried my hands deep in her hair, angling her face to mine as I captured her lips. Hot, needy kisses. "I will always love you," I barely whispered the words against the corner of her mouth.

Hailee rose up slightly, grasping my shaft in her hand before sinking down in one smooth motion. "Cam," she breathed, clutching onto my shoulders. "It feels—"

"I know," I groaned, rocking into her. My hand curved over her hip, guiding her movements. I wanted her slow and deep, fast and hard. I wanted her anyway I could get her. Because being like this with Hailee would never be enough... and yet, for now, it would have to be.

My chest tightened as she rode me. I memorized every roll of her hips, every breathy moan to fall from her lips. But I needed more. I needed every single thing she had to give.

Without warning, I flipped Hailee over and began thrusting into her. She raked her nails down my back, crying out as I went harder. "Oh God, Cam..." Sucking in a sharp breath, she held onto my shoulders as I chased that moment when everything else melted away and you were left with nothing but a feeling of complete ecstasy.

Hailee moaned again. "It's..."

Everything.

It was everything...

And it was goodbye.

Hailee

I woke up to an empty bed, but I hadn't expected Cameron to be here. We'd said all we needed to say last night, with every kiss and touch and whispered I-love-you.

I didn't doubt Cameron loved me; it was never about that. But I knew he couldn't be what he needed to be to his family while he felt tied to me.

So I set him free.

We hadn't discussed what would happen when I went back to Michigan. We hadn't discussed if we were on a break, or over, or going to try to do the long-distance thing.

We hadn't discussed anything.

But that told me all I needed to know.

Right now, Cameron's priority was his family, and I couldn't hate him for that.

No matter how much it hurt, I just couldn't.

"Sweetheart?" Mom's voice drifted through the door.

"Hey, Mom."

She peeked around the door. "How are you feeling this morning?"

"I'm okay."

"Did you and Cameron work through things?"

My cheeks heated. "Actually, I'm going to head back to Michigan later."

"Alone?" Confusion clouded her eyes.

"Cameron needs to be here."

"I know, sweetheart. I can't even imagine..." She perched on the edge of my desk. "But that sounds kind of final."

"We haven't worked out the details."

"And you're okay with this?"

I shrugged, dropping my gaze. "Cameron needs to be here for his family."

"Of course he does, but—"

"Mom, I appreciate your concern, I do. But it's done."

"You'll find your way back to one another. No amount of time or distance will ever change how that boy feels about you."

God, I wanted to believe her. But I also knew there was one thing that could change everything, and it was going to happen.

"Karen isn't going to get better, Mom." I couldn't hold the tears at bay any longer.

"Oh, sweetheart, I'm so, so sorry."

"Life is so unfair," I sobbed, falling into Mom's open arms.

"Ssh, sweetheart. I'm right here."

But as she said the words, I only cried harder, because one day soon, Cameron and Xander were going to have to say goodbye to their mom.

And Cameron would be left to pick up the pieces.

———

I flew back to Michigan after that. Mom and Kent gave me a ride to the airport, insisting that I call more often. They didn't like the idea of me being in Ann Arbor on my own, but there was something strangely comforting about returning to mine and Cameron's apartment.

It was so full of him. His Wolverine's hoodie on the coat rack, the sports column cuttings of all his mentions stuck to the noticeboard in the kitchen, right down to the lingering scent of his aftershave.

It hurt.

It hurt so much, but I wouldn't have wanted to be anywhere else.

Dropping my keys on the sideboard, I pulled out my cell phone and started a new message.

Me: Just got back to the apartment. Send my love to Xander, and your mom and dad xo

Cameron: I will, and thank you Hailee, for everything.

There was still so much we needed to discuss, questions that needed answering. But they could wait.

They would have to.

My cell phone began vibrating and I hit answer.

"We need to talk."

"Hello to you too, Jason."

"What the fuck, Hailee? You were supposed to fight, not walk away."

"That's not... I didn't walk away." *I let him go.*

"Cameron is confused. He doesn't know what the fuck he wants right now. But I'm telling you: He. Needs. You."

"And I'm here, I am. I'm not going anywhere, Jason, but I'm not going to be an added burden either."

"I can't believe he let you leave." The fight left my stepbrother's voice.

"Yeah..." My heart ached as if it knew it was missing its other half.

"How are you holding up?"

"I'm okay. I just keep thinking nothing I'm feeling matters, not compared to..."

"Yeah," his voice sobered, "I know. I offered to drive to Rixon, but he wouldn't even entertain the idea."

"Cameron needs to do things his way," I said.

"And if his way isn't the right way?"

"Then we'll pick up the pieces."

"You'll get through this. It can't be the end, Sis. It just can't."

"Maybe," I said with little conviction.

"Just don't write him off, not yet."

"Jason, I would never do that." *I love him too damn much.*

"Do you need anything? I can drive up and—"

"No, I'm okay." I smiled. Jason was so different, and I

was proud of the man he'd become. "Just take care of him, please."

"I will. He gets a couple of days and then I'm going down there."

"Good. He'll need someone to talk to."

"You're the best of us, Hailee, you know that, right?"

"Thank you." Emotion clogged my throat.

"I'll call you soon to check in."

"Okay, bye, Jas—" My stomach churned violently. "I need to go." I dropped the phone and raced through the apartment, crashing through the bathroom door just in time for my lunch to make a reappearance.

So much for a twenty-four-hour stomach flu.

26

Hailee

Cameron didn't return to school. He quit the team and deferred his classes. Jason had driven up last weekend to collect some of his things and take them back to Rixon.

That had been hard.

But it was for the best.

Doctors couldn't give the Chase family a clear prognosis. But they had told them to treasure every moment which didn't sound good.

We'd talked a couple of times, but we didn't talk about us. Instead, I told Cameron all about my latest art project and he told me about his quest to make sure Xander knew how loved he was.

It was hard to stay mad at a guy who cared so much.

Devyn checked on me a lot, as did some of the other football girlfriends. But mostly, I preferred my own company. Besides, I'd been unable to shake whatever virus I'd picked up. I wasn't ill all the time, but I still didn't feel right. So much so, Mom had begged me to get some blood work done.

I was heading to get my results from the doctor's office before flying to Philadelphia to meet Felicity and Mya for some girls' time. The guys were in Rixon with Cam and Xander for the weekend, so Mya had invited us to hang out.

"Miss Raine?" The secretary said, and I nodded. "You can go straight in." She smiled.

"Thank you."

I made my way down the hall and knocked on the door.

"Come in."

"Hello."

"Hailee, take a seat." Dr. Jennifer said. "How are you feeling today?"

"Okay. I'm still a little lethargic though. And I had another bout of nausea the other day."

"I'm not surprised."

"Excuse me?"

"We ran a full blood work up. Everything came back fine."

My brows furrowed. "I'm sorry, I don't understand. I thought you just said—"

"You're pregnant, Hailee."

"P- pregnant?" It *whooshed* from my lips. "But I can't be."

"I have the results right here. Your levels put you at around nine weeks."

"But I didn't miss my period."

"It's rare but it happens. Do you experience light periods?"

"Usually, yes."

She made some notes. "Is it possible you missed your birth control?"

"No, I take it religiously."

"Again, it happens. Obviously, you don't need to take that anymore."

"You're sure I'm pregnant?"

"Hailee, I know this is a shock..." She wasn't wrong about that. Pregnancy was the last thing I'd expected to hear her say. It was so far down the list, I hadn't even contemplated it.

"Is the father on the scene?"

"It's complicated." My hands trembled as I tried to process what she was saying. "I'm sorry, when would I have conceived?"

"If the dates are correct, and sometimes they're a little out, it would put it at about seven weeks ago."

My hand instinctively went to my stomach. "I'm really pregnant?" Tears burned the backs of my eyes, but I didn't know if they were tears of joy or despair.

"You are. I suggest buying yourself a couple of home test kits. It might provide the visual proof you need." Her smile was reassuring but it did little to ease the storm raging inside me.

"Here." She pulled out a leaflet and pushed it across the desk. "This explains what happens next. If you have any questions, don't hesitate to call the office."

"I'm flying."

"Excuse me?"

"Today. I'm flying to Philadelphia to meet some girlfriends."

"You should be fine, but if you've been feeling nauseous then the altitude might not help. And no alcohol."

"Of course."

"I'm going to write you a script for some pre-natal vitamins, check your blood pressure, and then you can be on your way. Any questions?"

"I.... uh. No, I think that's everything."

It wasn't.

But I didn't know where the hell to start.

Dr. Jennifer took my blood pressure, handed me the script, and wished me well. I walked out of there in a complete trance, unable to think of anything else...

I was *pregnant*.

————

I barely remembered the flight to Philadelphia. I hadn't gotten sick, I'd just been stuck in a paralyzing state of disbelief. It wasn't until Felicity was pulling me into her arms in the arrivals lounge that I finally snapped out of it.

"Hailee, what is it? What's wrong?"

"I'm pregnant," I blurted out, a stream of big, ugly sobs following.

"Okay." Her eyes went wide as she dug out her cell. "Mya," she said. "Change of plan. We need to stop at the store for supplies then head straight to your apartment. I'll tell you when we're out of arrivals." Felicity hung up. "Come on, babe. It sounds like we have some catching up to do."

She didn't push for answers on the ride to Asher and Mya's apartment, and I was grateful. I still needed to assimilate my thoughts on everything. But when we pulled into their underground parking lot, I knew my reprieve was up.

I climbed out of the car and went around to the trunk to get my bag, but Flick beat me to it. "I can carry my bag," I protested.

"Hush, you've got to think for two now."

I shot her a disapproving look.

"Too soon?"

"What do you think?"

"I think you need to explain how you're pregnant when you told me you and Cameron were going through a dry spell?"

"Seriously, *that's* what you're choosing to focus on?"

"Fee, you're doing it again," Mya said.

"Sorry, I'm sorry, okay." She held up a hand. "I just... pregnant. She's freakin' pregnant."

"Yes, I got it the first time." Mya offered me an apologetic look. "How are you feeling, really?"

"Confused. Scared. Did I say confused?"

"It's okay, Hailee. You're going through something huge."

"Have you told Cam?" That was Felicity. I pressed my lips together, averting my gaze. "Hailee... you have to tell him."

"I can't, not yet."

He was dealing with something huge; he didn't need this to worry about.

"Girl," Mya reached for my hand. "He'd want to know."

"I need to process it first and then figure out what I'm going to do."

"What do you mean?" Felicity paled. "You're going to keep it, right?"

"I..." I couldn't answer that question. My heart said yes. But... *a baby*?

Cameron and I weren't even together. Well, at least, I didn't think we were.

God. Everything was such a mess.

"I'm still in college. I want to graduate." Guilt coiled around my heart.

The elevator doors pinged open and we all filed out, heading for Mya's apartment.

"You can't be more than, what, two months along?"

"The doctor thinks I'm nine weeks."

"So you're due when, June?" Felicity asked, doing the math.

"June second."

"Perfect. You can take finals, graduate, and then have the baby."

"And where we will live? What about my plans?"

Her expression fell. "It's not straightforward, but you'll figure it out. Besides, Cameron will step up."

"I think Cameron has enough on his plate." My heart clenched again. Finding out I was pregnant was supposed to be a happy occasion. It wasn't supposed to happen now, in the middle of all this.

She rolled her eyes. "You can't seriously be thinking about keeping this from him because of what's happening with his mom?"

I blinked away the fresh tears.

"That's all the more reason to tell him. God knows, that family needs some good news."

"I'll think about it. But please, don't tell Asher or Jason yet. I need time."

"Hailee—"

"No, Fee, I mean it. I told you in confidence. This is my business. Please respect that."

She let out a little huff, but nodded. "My lips are sealed."

"Good." Because this wasn't some salacious secret that would cause a scandal. It was the kind of secret that changed lives.

I knew Cameron deserved to know, but I'd walked away to unburden him. If I told him now, I'd only be adding more responsibility to his shoulders.

At least that's what I kept telling myself, as I followed my friends into Asher and Mya's apartment.

Cameron

"What will happen to me when Mom dies?" Xander's words were like a punch to the stomach. I hugged him tighter, running my nose over his hair as I tried to swallow the ball of emotion lodged in my throat.

"You'll have me and Dad."

"What about Hailee?"

Fuck. He was really hitting me where it hurt today.

"Hailee and I are..." The truth was, I didn't know what we were anymore.

We talked and texted occasionally, and she sent Xander these cute little care packages. But we didn't talk about the elephant in the room.

Us.

When I'd found out Mom was sick again, I hadn't turned to Hailee. I couldn't. Instead, I'd steeled myself to be there for my family. Hailee needed to graduate. She needed to chase *her* dreams, and figure out what *she* wanted.

I'd always imagined that our life would end up back in Rixon one day. But not like this. Not because Mom was... I still couldn't say it.

"Did she go back to Michigan because of me?"

I pushed Xander out of my arms and lowered my face to his. "Hailee loves you, squirt. She loves you so much. But I need to be here with you, and Mom and Dad. And Hailee's life is in Michigan right now."

"But after college, she'll come back, right?"

I couldn't answer him, because I didn't have one.

I hadn't asked anything of Hailee since she'd gone back to Michigan, and she'd given me the space I needed.

But nothing about it felt right. I missed her every second of every day. I missed her so much, my soul ached for her.

"Hey, boys," one of the nurses came out of Mom's room. "She's all yours."

"Thanks," I said, pulling Xander up with me.

"Don't get too rowdy, okay? She's tired."

"We'll behave." I gave the nurse a weak smile.

Xander hesitated when we reached her door, but I gave

him a gentle nudge. He was doing better. Since I made the decision to stay in Rixon, my little brother no longer seemed so lost.

"There are my boys," Mom smiled, patting the bed.

"Go," I whispered to Xander, my heart swelling as I watched him fall into her arms and bury his face in her shoulder.

"Gosh, Xander, you get bigger every time I see you."

"Mom," he groaned, "It's been two days."

"Two days too many."

It was so good to see them together, even under the circumstances.

"How are you feeling?" I moved closer, leaning over my brother to press a kiss to her damp forehead.

"Okay." I heard the lie in her voice, but we didn't address it. We never did.

We'd made a promise—Mom, Dad, and I—that we needed to be strong for Xander. No matter how bad things got, we would shield him as much as possible.

"Are you hungry?" she asked Xander. "I heard they're doing tacos in the cafeteria today."

"I love tacos."

"I know you do, baby. You want to go with Dad and get some? He should be here any—"

"Did I hear someone say tacos?"

Mom chuckled and it was like music to my ears.

"Hey, Dad," Xander said.

"Hey, buddy. Shall we go feed you?"

"Don't be too long," Mom called after them. When

they were gone, she patted the bed again. "Come closer, sweetheart."

"Hey, Mom."

"I wanted to talk to you about something," she said, and my brows furrowed. "I had a dream last night, and I woke up with the strangest feeling..." She took my hand in hers. "I know you want to be here, and I love you for it, I do. But I think you need to go and see Hailee—"

"Mom..."

"Just hear me out. You know I'm not one for superstition, but I can't shake the feeling she needs you."

"If you're trying to make me feel guiltier than I already do, you're doing a pretty good job of it." I gave her a tight smile.

"Oh, Cameron, my sweet boy." She pressed her hand against my cheek. "Hailee is your heart. You can't live without your heart, baby."

"But Mom, I can't go..." Tears burned my throat. "What if something happens—"

"Ssh." Her eyes fluttered closed. "All I want is for you and Xander to be happy. That's all any mother can wish for. And that girl is your key to happiness. You need to let her in, Cameron. Love is hard and messy, and God knows, it hurts sometimes. But the kind of love the two of you share is rare. And I can't explain it, but she needs you right now. I just know it."

"But you need me..." The dam broke and tears spilled freely down my cheeks.

"I'm not going anywhere yet, I promise. I need to make

sure my boy pulls his head out of his butt and makes things right with his girl first."

"Okay," I breathed.

"Okay?"

"Yeah, Mom," I said, because how could I deny her?

How could I deny myself when all I wanted was to see Hailee, to know she was okay?

The answer was, I couldn't.

27

Hailee

I felt like crap.

Ever since finding out I was pregnant two weeks ago, it had been a constant cycle of sickness and lethargy. I'd missed a ton of classes, and spent most of my time camped out on the sofa watching daytime TV, sucking ice chips, and feeling sorry for myself.

Felicity and Mya were on my back to tell Cameron. According to my dates, I was almost entering the second trimester. I had a scan booked for next week.

I wanted to tell him. I did. So many times, I'd reached for my cell to call him. But every time, something stopped me.

Cameron was facing the biggest loss a child could have... the timing sucked.

Everything about it sucked.

Yet, I knew I had to tell him eventually.

I'd just got comfortable, ready for another episode of Friends, when the doorbell rang. That was odd. People usually buzzed to be let into the building.

Throwing the blanket off me, I padded across the apartment and checked the peephole. "Cameron?" His name spilled from my lips and I fumbled to open the door. "What are you doing here?"

"Hey." An uncertain smile tugged at the corner of his lips. "Can I come in?" he asked when I didn't reply.

"I... uh... this is your apartment too; you don't need an invitation."

Cameron was here.

Oh God.

I pulled my oversized cardigan around my body.

"Are you okay," he said, "you don't look so good?"

"I'm fine. What are you doing here?"

"I'm sorry to just show up, but my mom—"

"Is she okay? I mean, I know she's not okay. But did something—"

"Hailee, relax, she's okay, all things considered."

"That's good." I let out a small sigh of relief. "You didn't call to say you were coming?"

"Honestly?" He ran a hand down his handsome face. "I didn't know what to say."

"Oh."

This was so awkward, and I hated it. I hated that we'd become like strangers to one another.

"Do you want to sit?" I asked.

"Yeah, that would be good."

We moved into the living room. "Are you sure you're okay?" He eyed the glass of ice chips and the blanket.

"I haven't been feeling great."

"I didn't know."

"You've had bigger things on your mind. How's Xander?"

"He's good. Thank you for the care packages. He loved them. He misses you."

I gave him a small shrug. "It's the least I could do. Cameron, why are you here?" I blurted out.

"Sorry, I didn't mean—"

"That came out wrong. I'm happy to see you, I am. It's just you kind of caught me off guard."

"I miss you, Hailee. I miss you so fucking much. I wanted to call, but I was so scared you'd tell me not to come…"

"You thought I'd… Cameron, I'm right here. I've always been here. I've just been trying to give you space."

"I know you have." He reached for me, but thought better of it and thrust his hand under his thigh. It stung.

"My mom had a dream…"

"A dream?"

"I know it sounds crazy, but she got it into her head you needed me. She insisted I come to see you. Like got really weird about it."

"So, you're here because of your mom?"

"No, that's not… I know how it sounds, but I wanted to come. I've wanted to come ever since you left. But I couldn't leave them, and it wasn't fair to ask you to stay. Fuck…" Cameron's eyes shuttered as he inhaled a ragged breath. "Everything is so fucked-up."

Shuffling closer, I took his hand in mine, squeezing it gently. "It's okay. I understand."

"Do you?" His eyes slid to mine. "Because I don't. I don't understand anything anymore. But my mom said I needed to come, and it was like she was giving me permission... so here I am."

"Cameron..." I swallowed the words. It was like Karen was here, standing over us, watching as we tried to sort our shit out.

I knew if Cameron hadn't turned up here today, I probably wouldn't have told him yet. But could I really let him leave without giving him the truth?

"I don't understand either," I whispered. "But your mom was right."

"W- what do you mean?" His eyes were filled with trepidation.

"I'm pregnant."

The silence was deafening. My pulse hammered inside my chest, making me a little lightheaded.

"You're *pregnant*?"

I nodded. "Almost three months."

"But... how?"

"The doctor said it happens sometimes. I didn't miss a period, but I was sick when I came to Rixon with you, remember?"

"You knew and you didn't tell me?"

"I didn't think you'd be ready to hear it..." I still wasn't sure he was.

"The ice chips?"

"Morning sickness sucks." I went to pull my hand away, but Cameron caught it.

"A baby? We're having... *a baby*?" He swallowed, an awestruck expression falling over him.

It was too much, and tears sprang from my eyes as I nodded.

"I'm sorry." He dropped to his knees, moving between my legs. "I'm so fucking sorry. I should have been here. I should have been here with you."

"No." I brushed the hair from his eyes. "You needed to be with your family. I understand—"

"You're my family too, Hailee. I should never have pushed you away. I'm so sorry. She knew, my mom knew... how is that even possible?"

I didn't know, but I would be forever thankful to her.

"Maybe she just wants to make sure you're happy before she..."

Sadness washed over us both. "She said the same thing." Cameron curved his hand around the nape of my neck and touched his head to mine. "Can you forgive me?"

"There's nothing to forgive."

"I guess we have a lot to talk about," he said. "But first, I'd really like to kiss you."

I stared down at him, fighting a smile as I said, "What are you waiting for?"

Cameron

Six months later...

"I don't want to," Hailee cried, pain filling her voice.

I squeezed her hand. "Just another big push, and he'll be here."

My son.

I was having a son.

To say the last six months had been a whirlwind was an understatement. After Mom had sent me to Michigan, Hailee and I started making plans for the future. We got to enjoy one last Christmas with my mom. It had been bittersweet, but we'd filled it with so much love and happiness and gifts, all the gifts, that it was hard to look back and be sad. Mom had gotten her wish. I was happy, Xander was doing better, and my son was about to make his grand entrance into the world.

"Okay, Hailee, he's almost here. I need you to push again, okay?"

"Cam, I can't do it." She turned into me and I kissed her damp forehead.

"You've got this, Hailee. One more push."

Her screams filled the room but then a different sound took over. A baby's cries.

"He's here," I choked out. "He's finally here."

It had been hard losing Mom three months ago. We'd all hoped she would make it to see the baby, but in the end it wasn't meant to be. I'd made a promise to her that he would know his Grandma Karen though. He would know of her love and strength and spirit.

Tears rolled down my cheeks as the nurses handed Hailee the bundle of blankets. "Oh God, Cam," she croaked. "Look at him."

I stroked a finger along his little face. "He's perfect."

"He really is."

As I watched Hailee watch our son, I was hit with such a sense of pride and love, I felt sure I would combust.

"Have you decided on a name?" I asked her, my voice shaky with emotion.

"Avery Chase, after your mom."

It had been her middle name.

"I love you," I said. "I love you both so much and I will spend my life loving you."

"We know." Hailee smiled, her eyes filled with so much happiness I just knew we were going to be okay.

Because if my mom had taught me anything, it was that life didn't always go to plan. We couldn't know what was around the corner, we could only live each moment as it came. And I intended on loving each and every moment for her.

For my son, and my family.

For the girl who had stolen my heart when I was just a boy.

I'd live it for them all.

Because I'd been taught once to play hard... fight hard... and *love* hard.

EPILOGUE

"It's official folks. Fans everywhere will be mourning the loss of one of the greats today. Jason Ford, Heisman Trophy winner, American All-Star, and one of the NFL's top-rated quarterbacks of all-time is retiring. After six years with the Philadelphia Eagles, Ford suffered a string of injuries last season."

"Yeah, Dan, it's been a rocky year for the record-breaking QB. He enjoyed five years of success with the Eagles, including two super bowls, but last year he suffered that nasty shoulder cuff injury and things went downhill pretty quickly from there."

"But his high school team, the Rixon Raiders will be pretty excited to see the return of Ford as he joins them as assistant coach."

"That's right, Dan. Ford and his family are relocating back to Rixon. And who knows, maybe it won't be the end of his legacy."

Jason

There had once been a time when a three-year-old's birthday party would have sent me running for the hills. But when one of the birthday girls was your daughter, that wasn't really an option. I cut the engine, climbed out of my SUV, and set about emptying the trunk of all the balloons Fee and Hailee had sent me out to get.

Fuck knows why we needed more balloons. Cam's house was already full of the damn things. But I knew better than to argue with my wife *and* my sister.

Hands full, I trudged up the driveway, which was already full of cars, and let myself into the house. It sounded like a zoo, kids running and screaming, adults hovering on the fringes unsure whether to intervene or let them have at it.

God, I missed football.

At least back then, things were simple.

"Daddy, Daddy," Lily charged at my legs. "You got boons."

"Sure did, baby." I thrust the handful of balloons at the first person I saw and scooped up the birthday girl. "Are you enjoying your party?"

"Yes," she shrieked with glee. "I am free."

"Three, you're three, Lily."

"She's a handful, is what she is." Fee came over with our youngest, Poppy, asleep in her arms, and leaned in kissing Lily, and then my cheek. "Thank you."

"Anything for the birthday girls. This place is crazy." I eyed my wife discreetly. Three-year old's were cunning things, wily and intuitive. Cam kept telling me it was a girl thing, which meant I was shit out of luck since I had two daughters. At least he had Xander and Avery to balance things out.

Lucky fucker.

Guilt flashed through me. Cameron was lucky. He had a beautiful family, but it had come at a steep price. Three years after his mom had died, Clarke, his dad, had been killed in a traffic accident. He and my sister had become Xander's guardians after that, their family of three turning into four. Then Hailee found out she was pregnant again. Now they had their hands full trying to raise a teenager, a six-year-old, and a three-year-old.

But they made it look easy. Hailee loved being a mom and Cameron was so good with the kids, I was a tad jealous.

"There's my beautiful niece." Hailee approached us. "Where's my cuddle, Lil?"

"Auntie Ailee." Lily reached for my sister and I let her go.

"Where's Cam and Ash?" I asked her, hooking my arm around Fee's waist.

"The last time I saw Asher, he was trying to wrestle the twins upstairs for a diaper change."

"That I would pay to see."

"Babe," Fee warned, pressing her hand to my stomach. "He's trying his best. But twins are..." She shuddered.

"Yeah, I can't even imagine."

"Good, because I'm done. Two is more than enough for us." She grinned up at me and I captured her lips in a kiss.

"I'm going to find the men." In my experience, you

needed to stick together at these things, otherwise the little monsters would divide and conquer.

———

I found Cameron hiding in Hailee's studio. Ashleigh was asleep on his shoulder. "Hey," I whispered. "Too much for the birthday girl?"

Lily and Ashleigh were born only days apart, so we usually celebrated together.

"She just crashed like ten minutes ago. I don't want to disturb her."

"It's crazy out there."

"It's life." He took a long pull on his beer. "I can't believe they're three already." He gazed at his daughter.

"How did we end up here, man?"

"End up where?" Asher joined us.

"Here in a house full of screaming kids."

"Don't look at me," he said, perching against the sideboard. "I don't even know what day it is right now."

"You should just come home," Cam suggested. "Move back to Rixon and let your folks help out with the twins."

"We're thinking about it."

"Yeah?" I asked.

"Yeah. Mya's aunt is sick, and she wants to be closer to her. But we've got to think of the kids."

Mya and Asher had fostered six kids over the last few years. I didn't know how they did it, but they made it work.

"You can still foster in Rixon."

"We can, but you know how Mya feels about being in the city."

"It would be good to have you both back, the kids can grow up together..."

"Fuck, can you imagine?" I liked to live in denial about having daughters... daughters who would one day become *teenage girls*.

"Do you ever think it's karma for all the bad shit we did back in the day?" My eyes went to my niece still sleeping soundly on her daddy's shoulder.

"Karma?" Cam chuckled. "You think having daughters is karma?"

"I'm not ready for it."

"For what?"

"School..." My jaw clenched. "All those little punks thinking they can—"

"Jase, they're three."

"Yeah, and one day they'll be seventeen thinking they can tame the bad boy."

"You've really given this a lot of thought, haven't you?" Asher smirked, and I flipped him off.

"You're telling me you haven't thought about it? Remember what we were like in high school? What Hailee, Mya, and Fee were like." I glared at both of them and realization slowly dawned on their expressions.

"We're fucked," Cam said.

"Totally fucked." Asher ran a hand down his face.

"Welcome to my world," I grumbled.

There had once been a time I'd thought football was

everything... but football was the dream. This right here, this was the life.

It was everything.

Every-fucking-thing.

ACKNOWLEDGEMENTS

It feels like it's the end of an era... except, the next generation are coming!!!

Originally, when I planned this series, I planned three books. But a wonderful thing happened, readers wanted more. More Cam and Hailee, more Jase and Flick, more Asher and Mya... The Endgame Is You was only supposed to be a short peek into their futures (and an opportunity to introduce their children), but it became so much more. I fell hopelessly back into their world, and I'll be honest, I'm a little sad it had to end.

But when one door closes, another opens. And I hope you'll stick around to read about Lily, Poppy, Ashleigh, Sofia, and Aaron.

Thank you for loving these characters, for embracing their stories, and for wanting more.

As always, it takes a village to publish a book, and this one is no different.

Huge thanks to my whole team (editor, alpha and beta readers, my authors pals, my proofreaders, audio narrators, and foreign publishers). I feel blessed to work with such incredible people. But just a few quick special mentions...

Andie, you rock my socks! I gave you a crazy deadline

and you STILL managed to get it back to me before the final hour... there really aren't enough thank yous!

Nina, you've been with this series from the beginning and I'm so grateful. I hope I did your boys justice.

To my beta readers: Annissia, Heather, and Cassie, thank you for reading the story as I wrote it and for all your helpful feedback!

And to every single reader, blogger, and bookstagrammer who has supported this story – I get to do this job because of you. So thank you!

Until next time,

L A xo

ABOUT THE AUTHOR

ANGSTY. EDGY. ADDICTIVE ROMANCE

Author of mature young adult and new adult novels, L A is happiest writing the kind of books she loves to read: addictive stories full of teenage angst, tension, twists and turns.

Home is a small town in the middle of England where she currently juggles being a full-time writer with being a mother/referee to two little people. In her spare time (and when she's not camped out in front of the laptop) you'll most likely find L A immersed in a book, escaping the chaos that is life.

L A loves connecting with readers.

The best places to find her are
www.lacotton.com

Printed in Great Britain
by Amazon